The Martian Ones

Tales of Human Folly

by

Gabriel Hugo

Mission, Texas

Copyright **2018**

ISBN-13: 978-0998996516

ISBN-10: 0998996513

The Martian Ones: Tales of Human Folly

Copyright holder: Gabriel H. Sanchez

Editor & Book Design: Gabriel H. Sanchez

**Front and Back Cover Art by:
Hugo K. Sanz, a.k.a. The Artist Known as 'Hu'
www.theartofhu.com**

Introducing the Tales of Human Folly

(A brief synopsis)

In 2018 visionaries like Elon Musk wanted to go to Mars. They wanted to give humanity a chance to bounce back as a species after the anticipated apocalypse. But they failed to foresee that now, in 2081, Dr. Damian Martin has perverted that vision of the continuity of humankind. He has created a hybrid species based on human and Martian DNA. These creatures have the power to communicate telepathically with one-another, transform from alien to human so as to blend in among other people, and Dr. Martin has the full intention to conquer the human race with his secret army of alien/human hybrids. Only one woman stands a chance to stop this mad scientist. Her name is Captain Ana Rodriguez. But even she seems strangely connected to the Martian Ones by some strange ability to participate in their telepathic communication. She feels strangely affected by, and invested in, these creatures' well-being. And there is no telling if she will turn the tide against Dr. Martin's plans, since he has taken as insurance for her cooperation the thing she holds dearest to her heart...her own daughter.

Back on Mars, and perhaps on an alternate universe, a colony has been established that has lasted decades and seems to be thriving. It all looked to be going as planned until one day someone spotted a stranger in the distance approaching the colony. Could it be a real Martian? It turned out that it was none other than a member of the colony whom people had presumed dead, since she had been missing for quite some time. But there she was at their doorstep. Most alarming and thought-provoking was the fact that she had apparently survived the Martian landscape without a functioning oxygen suit. How was this possible? Only one of two explanations are initially explored: either she was saved by a miracle, or she was an android programmed to think that she and all of her companions were humans settling Mars. There is a possible third alternative explanation; one which is the most frightening... that they had been living a simulated life.

On yet another alternate reality, humanity's first four pioneers were two men and two women. They had left Earth each for their own personal reasons involving their pursuit of the stars but also to escape certain pitfalls of life on the home planet. Such was the case for Karina, the youngest of the crew. She had been adopted as a child after having crossed into the U.S. as an unaccompanied minor. Karina demonstrated she was committed to her country and to excellence, which was why she had been selected to join the crew that would establish the first Martian colony. But her personal reason for leaving Earth, aside from her professional aspirations, was a deeply personal one, which involved a troubled and dark experience with members of the opposite sex in her family. This had been what had prompted her to leave her birthplace of El Salvador in Central America and would eventually lead to her eagerness to join the Martian colonizing crew. But Karina had not counted on the fact that the errors of man follow him where ever he may go, be it to the United States, or to Mars. And so, on Martian soil, Karina was forced to deal once and for all with the evil side of man that had plagued her life. In doing so, though she ensures that humanity's first colony on Mars is a complete failure, she is able to free herself at last and travel beyond Mars to a place where she may finally find the change she sought to see in her fellow men.

These and other stories make up what are referred to as the "Tales of Human Folly". This collection of dystopian fiction addresses the question of the possibilities and barriers humans face on Earth and on any other part of the universe. It begs the question, "If human cannot unite and work together on Earth to reach new interstellar heights, how will they conquer other worlds?" Only time will tell if human beings are destined to occupy outer space. Unfortunately, time is running out on Earth.

...According to the Bulletin of Atomic Scientists, in 2018 the "DOOMSDAY CLOCK" stands at 2 minutes to midnight.

Dedication

In 2018, thousands of families are fleeing the only world that they had ever known in countries of Central America and are coming to the United States to find a better, safer place to establish themselves and start again with renewed hope and dreams of a better future.

This book is dedicated to a future Chicanx little girl or boy who may grow up to save humanity by helping colonize Mars and worlds beyond.

.

Artist's rendition based on eyewitness accounts.
July 4, 2081

Table of Contents

The Martian Ones

The door swung wide open allowing a flood of fluorescent, blue light emanating from the hallway into the dimly-lit room where Captain Rodriguez waited alone, plagued with questions, wondering what she was doing there. A man of sizable stature and a full head of grey hair entered the room bearing two Styrofoam cups, one in each hand. His face was marked by heavy wrinkles that implied his age—just over seventy years old—however his towering figure, fully erect, looked surprisingly young and imposing. He was Dr. Damian Martin, Director of the Mars program at World Space Command. He approached the table and sat opposite the Captain, close to the door.

"Hello, Captain Rodriguez. How are you holding up?" He asked, still holding the cups in his hands.

"Not too good. What am I doing here? Why am I being held?" said the Captain turning her eyes toward him in an underhanded motion.

"You are not being held. We just need to clear some things before you all return back to your civilian lives."

"You mean my whole team is being held, too?"

"Again, you are not being *held*. It is standard

procedure to—"

"I am familiar with standard procedure, sir… With all due respect. It wasn't my first rodeo, you know? Me and my team have been on quite a few of these missions. This is NOT standard procedure. We are being held against our will and I demand to know why."

The director's eyes shot up from the table as he was placing the cups down and turned to look at the Captain.

"I understand this is uncomfortable for you, Captain. After all, it's not the liveliest of rooms. But, you must forgive us. We couldn't afford to compromise the entire compound."

He paused to look at her intently, not to allow her input but to quiet her down with a cold stare. After a short, awkward moment he said,

"I'm afraid we are getting ahead of ourselves. Why don't we start with you telling me all about the mission."

"What is there to tell? You all have the data we streamed from the live feed as it happened. And whatever else took place we revealed in our debriefing upon arrival."

"I'm sure you did. But, you see, there was a problem with the transmission. It wasn't very reliable. So, you can understand why I insist on hearing the entire version of events from your own mouth. That is, in your own words.

What did you see?"

"Look," Captain Rodriguez leaned over the table closer to the director until their faces were just inches apart and continued in a slow, deliberate manner, "I really don't know what more light I can shed for you on what went down. Like I said, everything that happened you guys know all about it. I imagine that you more than anybody else have access to every last second of our feed and my report, and all my team's eye-witness testimony. I would only be wasting your time telling you what you already know."

It was blatantly obvious to the director at this point that, though she was a lot younger, petite, and a woman, Captain Rodriguez was not the sort of underling he could intimidate easily with his overbearing presence and rank. He gave her a quick smirk.

"Yes, yes. It is true," said the director leaning back as he crossed one leg over the other and rested his hands over his knee as he exhaled calmly.

"I have access to any and all files available. But I am a meticulous man. And I prefer to hear things straight from the source. In person. So why don't you just tell me every single detail. Like telling it to someone who has no background knowledge in these matters."

Captain Rodriguez sighed in acquiescence and mirrored the director leaning back on her chair as well.

"Ok. If you insist," she said, shaking her head. "You're the boss. Don't say I didn't warn you if the story ends up being a snooze fest."

"No need to concern yourself with that. Why don't we just sit here and pretend that we are enjoying a nice cup of coffee outside of a quaint café on a nice, breezy day," he said, pushing the Styrofoam cup with the lukewarm liquid toward her. The Captain quipped in a sarcastic undertone,

"It's kind of hard to pretend to be enjoying a cup of coffee out in the open when you are holed up in a windowless room."

"Humor me," he responded dryly.

"Ok then," she exhaled, resigning herself to going along with this man until the moment could come for her to ask her own set of questions.

It was supposed to be a simple search and rescue job. We were to go to Mars as only the second crew to ever travel there. And we were to look for survivors of the original pioneer colony. Something had gone terribly wrong. World Space Command had lost all communication with them and thought that the entire crew had perished. But after some time, a vague, encrypted message reached Earth. It was a sign of hope that maybe some of the colonists had survived.

The night before liftoff, the mission commanders

came to our trailer out by the beach. After a big barbecue dinner and some drinks, they gathered us all together to run the details by us one more time. We were to explore the colony and try to find any survivors. That was the primary goal. However, we were also to look for possible causes for the colony's mission failure. The run-through of our objectives was pretty standard. Except when we got to the part where we were expected to carry around these huge, semi-automatic rifles. Not that handling weapons was outside of our expertise. If you ever had to assemble a team of weapons and combat specialists for a high stakes mission, you could not get a better one than me and my crew. But these guns were totally new to us. And besides, I had always been under the impression that there was nothing on Mars that could challenge or compromise our mission in the form of a foreign entity looking for trouble.

Nonetheless, when the top guys are telling you this is what you are going to do and this is what you are going to take as part of your gear, we tend not to get too picky about the ifs, hows, and whys. As a matter of fact, after my initial skepticism, I began to justify the need for weapons myself. What if the very colonists themselves became a mortal threat to us? We would definitely need some way to pacify them. Say what you will, but these people had already spent several years on a totally different planet. The first ones to ever do so. No one

5

could tell the exact ramifications of this reality. Who knew how being so alone, so far away from Earth could affect their psychological wellbeing, right? In any given situation, if it comes down to me or another person, you better believe I have no problem choosing me to win every time. Hands down. And I would use any and all means necessary, too."

"Admirable, Captain. You are decisive. Very good," Dr. Martin chimed in unexpectedly.

Captain Rodriguez seemed to snap out of a trance. She gave the director a puzzled look for having interrupted her as she was becoming completely immersed in her story.

"Forgive me. Please proceed," said the doctor coolly.

"As I was saying, several months later we were touching down on Mars. World Space Command directed us to land several miles outside the base so as to arrive unannounced and have complete control of all possible scenarios. But right from the start, as we exited the ship, I noticed the road leading to the colony looked a lot more tread-on than would seem possible. After all, these folks had not even been there more than a decade and there were only a few of them altogether. All in all, there were supposed to be twenty crew members, men and women. And they sure as hell had not brought more

than a couple of vehicles for transport. It was odd, but I said nothing to my crew and just ordered our march to our destination.

It was night fall when we arrived in the outskirts of the colony. We could only see the silhouettes of large hills from a distance. But I was certain it was the Martian base we were looking for. Yet that, too, made me pause an instant. The colony seemed much bigger than would be needed for such a small crew of settlers. These structures we were approaching looked capable of accommodating hundreds of people, not just the handful that we knew of. And when we arrived at the front side of the main building something told me that these facilities had been inactive for quite some time. So far, this whole mission to Mars had been one series of question after unanswered question. But I was not going to dwell on that and have my crew distracted on the oddities of our mission.

We had to override the access panel to open the entrance to the building. It was dark outside by then so we all made proper use of our standard issue flashlights mounted on top of our rifles. Once inside I divided the crew into smaller units. Linda and Eric down one corridor. Rosa and Julian down the opposite side. Daniel and I headed down the main hallway. We went room by room. Lab by lab. We checked everywhere. Like

I said before, everything looked like it had not been used in a while. Dusty and untouched. As if it had been years since there had been people making use of those facilities, not a few months like we had been told. After some time exploring that gigantic complex I heard one of my crew calling out. It was Eric. Based on the urgency in his voice which flooded my helmet I knew that they had found something unexpected.

'You're going to want to see this, Captain. Unbelievable.'

We rushed to their location. Rosa and Julian joined us shortly after. As we entered the room I found both Linda and Eric frozen in place. Rifles and flashlights fixed on a target, as if expecting to unload on it. I tapped Eric on the shoulder and he moved aside never once taking his eyes off the mark. I adjusted my eyes in the light and saw a silhouette at first. Then a dark shadow. And finally, I saw a man scared witless staring back at me. He had long, nappy hair. A long, scruffy beard on his face told me he had been surviving there possibly for months. Maybe even years.

'My name is Captain Ana Rodriguez with the World Space Command Marine Special Forces,' I said in a loud voice. The man seemed unaffected. No reaction. Just a spooked look on his face that wouldn't budge. Like he was having trouble believing his eyes. Perhaps

imagining instead that we were simply a hallucination. A trick of his mind.

I put down my weapon and approached. Rosa and Julian snugged up behind me and we walked in tandem. They kept their weapons and lights trained on the man. I took a knee beside him grabbing the man by the shoulders and shook him saying,

'What is your name? What was your post on this base?'

'Post? My post? Post...' He kept repeating the same words like a parrot, his gaze looking around at nothing in particular; a pair of lost eyes.

'What's your name?' I shouted at him shaking him harder. He shrugged his shoulders and shoved me away.

'Name! Name!' He grabbed his chin as if thinking hard. 'No name. No... No name...'

'Listen to me. We are here to help you. I'm going to need for you to pull it together and focus. Is there anyone else here besides you?'

The man's wild array of hand movements and gestures seemed to freeze as he heard my question. His eyes opened so wide it looked like the eyeballs would pop out. He was about to say something when a loud thump sounded off in another room. This startled him

9

*greatly, as if it were something familiar...something
terrifying. He grabbed me by the arms as if seeking
shelter.*

*I quickly glanced over at Julian and motioned for
him to go check out the source of the noise. Julian moved
out onto the hallway, cautiously approaching the next
door down. Over our helmets we could hear him report
shortly after leaving: 'Captain, we got movement.
Definitely something here.'*

*Before I could assign Linda to assist Julian while
I continued attempting communication with the wild
man, we heard a series of gunshots. I quickly signaled
for Rosa, Linda, and Eric to come with me, leaving
Daniel with the bewildered man.*

*I was first to reach the entrance to the room. We
moved in quick, guns at the ready. Julian turned to us
and cautioned for silence touching his index finger to his
helmet at the level of his lips then pointing it to a
counter. The whole team simultaneously aimed our
lights in that direction and approached cautiously. As we
turned a corner of the counter ready to shoot, I noticed a
shifting ball of flesh; little bodies crouching together,
hiding their faces away. Only one dared raise its head to
look in the direction of the lights. It was a group of
children. Badly kempt. Poorly nourished. They were
visibly afraid and timid. I put away my gun and
approached the group with arms extended downward
showing the palms of my hands. The children tightened
their circle wincing and screeching, each trying to
occupy the center where perhaps the feeling of safeness*

10

was more pronounced. But one by one they began to relax and look up at me slowly making my way to them with open arms, like the paintings of the Virgin Mary my mother hung up on our living room walls when I was a child.

I looked at Julian and said, 'They're just children, man!'

'Cap,' he said abbreviating my title. 'I swear that's not what I saw when I came in here. You should have seen 'em. There were these two weird things running around here. Big, red eyes glowing. They hissed and growled like animals. I shot at them. I'm pretty sure I clipped one, but they didn't seem bothered by my bullets. I think they just didn't like the brightness of my flash light. They got really annoyed when I shined the light directly at them,' said Julian in self-defense.'

I turned my attention back to the kids. I must have appeared much like a mother figure as I felt myself relaxed, safe. I don't know why. Those children just triggered something in me. I guess I have always secretly been a nurturer, even though that was not a side of me that my team and colleagues had ever witnessed. But I am sure you know very well, being that you guys do your homework to an extreme when you are vetting people like me, that I lost my only daughter when she was just three years old. I guess I never fully recovered. And the need to give that little person my love and affection never went away, either. I suppose it was what hurt the most about losing my daughter. I had all that warmth and love and nowhere to put it. That and the fact

11

that I will never get to see her grow to be the strong and independent woman that I know she would have become. That whole history was something I have always kept well hidden, knowing that an effective team led by a woman would only remain so if they felt their leader was a tough, strong person who could kick ass at a moment's notice without hesitation. A characteristic not aligned with a motherly figure devastated by the loss of a child.

The naked and scared children began to loosen up their tight, protective circle as they opened up and their little faces began to appear in the light. Their tiny eyes looked only to me, seemingly ignoring the presence of the rest of my team. They surrounded me and locked me in a tight embrace, as all children do with their parents when they have felt scared, seeking reassurance. I felt a strange sensation running through me in that very moment. It was the distinct impression that I was immersed in flight. My feet seemed to lift off the ground. My mind began to wander as if reaching the edge of consciousness, getting ready to enter into a dream. But before I could decipher what that feeling was, an abrupt sound brought me straight back to consciousness. It was Rosa shouting,

'Stop right there!'

I looked at Rosa picking up my gun.

'We've got company, Captain,' she said.

I signaled my team to be on the ready. Then in the darkness two sets of big, red eyes popped out of nowhere and flickered. No one waited for orders. Everyone squeezed their triggers, including me, shooting at two very rapidly moving shadows in the pitch-black room. After a very brief moment shooting at what seemed like ghosts, we paused and everything was calm, but no bodies on the floor to account for our spent ammo. In my helmet, I heard Daniel's voice come in:

'Cap'n, what's going on over there? You need assistance?'

'No. Stay where you are. We are coming to you,' I responded.

We retreated slowly with the children back to the room where Daniel appeared anxious to see what the whole fuss was about. I could sense he was also eager to be relieved from the duty of supervising the unintelligible rumblings of the anonymous Martian man. As we came in, however, the man noticed the children with me and became noticeably erratic, shouting and cursing at them. He stood up in a flash and attempted to run away but was stopped cold by Daniel. In a quick scuffle, he managed to wrestle Daniel's gun from his hands and raised it at the kids, shooting off just a few rounds over their heads. Luckily Rosa and Julian instinctively eliminated the threat before he could adjust his aim and hit the children—or us—shooting him down without hesitation.

For my part, I was really pissed by this sudden turn of events; upset because we could not help him, and because I would have wanted to claim him as part of my

13

human cargo from our Mars search and rescue mission. But, since there's no point crying over spilled milk, I decided to overlook some of the loses and focus on sweeping the entire facility in hopes of confronting the unknown creatures again. There was no doubt in my mind that those things were the cause of the original colonists' failed mission. Capturing one of them to bring back to Earth would have been icing on the cake. The question that came to mind later, however, was why had only the children been spared? With the sole exception of the bearded man, of course. I added that to the list of mysteries and unanswered questions about the Martian colony and went ahead with the task at hand.

I sent Julian to escort the children back to the rover and guard them while we swept room by room. Surprisingly, we could not find even a trace of those shadows that had lurked in the darkness, spying on us. Soon, I decided we could stay no longer. We would be risking losing even more lives if we did. I always look out for the safety of my crew. But this time it was the lives of those children that seemed to weigh heavier on my mind. So, we drove back to the ship and got ready to take off. Those children stuck to me like glue all throughout the trip. No one else seemed to exist to them. They said nothing neither to me or anyone else. I don't believe they can speak, to tell you the truth."

Captain Rodriguez paused, looked down at the palms of her hands, as if inspecting them for some kind of residue, then looked back up at the director.

"But that's all there is to tell," she said. "Now it's

14

my turn to ask the questions. What didn't you tell us about our mission, Dr. Martin? Because that story you all gave us was complete bull crap, wasn't it?"

"There is nothing else to tell, Captain. You did your part and for that we are grateful. Any other information regarding the failed Martian colony is top secret. I'm afraid I cannot share it with you. But thank you for your service. Even though you did lose a very valuable member of that colony. That wild man seemingly babbling nonsense was none other than our lead scientist overseeing our entire Mars operations. One Dr. Edgar J. Ruby. Rescuing him would have been of great use for the future of our program. Not to mention an almost guaranteed successful return to Mars and reinstatement of the colony. So, you see, Captain…perhaps you are not as good a leader of men as you think. That will be noted, Captain. It will definitely be noted. Now if you'll excuse me."

He rose to his feet and was about to leave, cutting their conversation abruptly but she stopped him in his tracks.

"You tell me what's going on. You tell me right now! Or else I will go to the media. I will go to the government watch groups. I will go to anyone who will listen and I will tell them what I have seen. It's obvious you are hiding something. Where's the rest of my crew? And the children? What happened at the Mars settlement?"

An alarm broke through the intercom, interrupting Captain Rodriguez's interrogation of her superior as it sounded off loudly, reverberating on that room's walls. The director took out his phone and called someone apparently within the compound. He shouted,

"Status report!" He squinted as he tried to listen over the loud alarm still blaring in the background. "Okay. Begin lockdown and full emergency procedures. Get everyone on it. Now!"

He looked at the Captain.

"You want to know the full story, don't you? Are you sure it's what you really want?" He shouted over the alarm.

"There is nothing I want more," responded Captain Rodriguez as the alarm abruptly shut off leaving her yelling in that unexpected silence.

"Captain," said the director. "Haven't you ever heard the expression 'Be careful what you wish for?' Some things are better off left uncovered. Some things you just can't come back from once you cross a certain limit."

"Cut the bullshit, Doctor. I'm a grown damn woman. I can take good care of myself. The void of space didn't even come close to spooking me like the void in my soul after losing my little girl and even that didn't break me. Nothing here on earth or in space is going to scare me."

"Very well. Your choice, Captain. Come with me," he said motioning at her with a *come-hither* finger.

They walked down a hall. Guards and other personnel were rushing past them fully armed toward a room at the end of the corridor where there appeared to be an exchange of gun fire. Surprisingly, though, the director

16

did not seem rushed and simply walked casually. The Captain followed suit.

As they neared the room she saw that the guards had not been shooting bullets, but instead they had been using special weapons that shot nets at a group of strange beings, trapping them and stopping them in their tracks. The creatures had dark grey skin, no hair, oval-shaped heads, sharp teeth visible through their terrible grins, and oversized red, glowing eyes. Height was hard to determine, because they were subdued and curled up in a ball writhing and hissing, but about four feet on average. It seemed the nets tightened further the more they wriggled in attempts to free themselves.

Doctor Martin looked around at his men and signaled one of them to approach. He placed his hand on the man's shoulder and said,

"Go in there and make sure those nets are secure enough so we may enter."

The man simply nodded and entered the room. The director stepped forward and shut the door behind him forcefully. Through a reinforced, thick glass window, which made up what would be the wall of that room extending from ceiling to floor, Captain Rodriguez could see that the man who was now locked-in with those monsters seemed to immediately comprehend the doctor's motivations, confused and afraid at the sudden realization of his troubles. He ran toward the door shouting for help to no avail. He looked at the director as if pleading and begging and asking why him? Then a look of anger and despise came over his face and he lifted his gun from its

17

holster shooting at the director only to see the bullets bounce off the reinforced glass. As he squeezed off a few rounds, two of the creatures' nets loosened up enough to allow them freedom to rise from the floor. They appeared to revel in the idea that live prey had joined them in their captivity. Slowly the creatures crept up to the petrified man like two ravenous Velociraptors aching to satiate themselves with flesh. In a last-ditch effort to save himself, the man shot at the monsters, but in spite of the impact of bullets, and with a quick pounce, they both latched onto him instantly tearing the man to pieces, eating him alive. His screams seemed to arouse the rest of the creatures still trapped in nets on the floor, no doubt eager to share a bite. That man's death cries made the hairs on the back of Captain Rodriguez's neck rise as she cringed at the sight.

"What the hell are those things? Are those… Chupacabras?" asked the Captain in awe. Within her deep, inner mind vague images floated around as she wondered why those red eyes looked familiar. They seemed to resemble the eyes she had encountered on Mars, though she had not been able to see the accompanying bodies on that occasion.

The director stood stoically as he observed the scene. He seemed oblivious to the Captain's inquiry. Or perhaps he simply ignored the question. But moments later he responded nonchalantly:

"That is the common name given to them. Yes. But look closely. Don't they seem a bit more familiar to you, Captain?"

The Captain tilted her head and peered into the

room through the window as she observed closely those strange beings on the floor and the other two now busily licking up the splotches of blood and guts from their midnight snack.

"What are you talking about?" she asked honestly perplexed.

"It's your cargo, Captain. Your human cargo. The children you rescued from the Martian base. In other words, the actual and sole reason you and your team were sent to Mars in the first place."

"No way. That can't be true. What happened to them?"

"I like to think of it as high-speed evolution. You see, these creatures are clearly not human beings. Although they do possess certain human traits. They are genetically engineered, or rather, modified. They are World Space Command's version of Adam and Eve. We are building a new race, Captain. One suited much better for the colonization and conquest of not just Earth and Mars, but all the galaxy and beyond!"

"So, you lied to us just to recover your experimental... things from Mars? What happened to the people on that base? Were they overrun by these creatures?"

"Well, we can't know that for sure, being that we don't have a reliable witness to what truly happened, do we?" The director said this throwing in the Captain's face the fact that she had lost his top scientist during her search and rescue mission.

"But if that were the case," he continued, "it would not have happened had it not been for human error. Precisely what we are trying to eliminate by creating this new species before us. They are ruthless. They are mission-oriented. And more importantly, they function most cohesively when they have found an adequate leader to lead them. As you know these creatures are not new on Earth. The reason people suspected their existence in the first place was because initially our program was based here on Earth. At one point, we had a situation here in which someone decided to try to expose us to the public. They broke protocol and attempted to escape with a few of the specimens. Unfortunately for that individual, we caught up with him quickly and disposed of him on the spot. But by then the harm had been done. The creatures had been released into the wild. That's when reports began to show up on the news of cattle being mutilated mysteriously."

"So, what happened to those creatures that escaped?"

"Eventually, we did recover them. But by then they had reached maturity and proved to be as stubborn as mules. We could no longer mold them into a cohesive unit. Sadly, we had to destroy them and start all over. Well, most of them, anyway.

"Let me get this straight. This whole time the entire Mars program has been simply to further this horrible experiment?"

"Of course not. This is a super-secret program, Captain. NASA and the other world agencies carry out their silly, idealistic missions into orbit selling a pipe dream to the general public. But World Space Command has a grander vision. A destiny. To take humanity to the next level in our evolution. Not NASA, nor those dreamers at the Mars Four Corporation, nor any of the various partner governments and agencies across the world know the true mission for Mars. I guess you could say this is 'our baby'."

The Captain simply stared at the creatures in the room as she sorted through all the thoughts in her head. This revelation was far beyond anything she had expected. And to think that she had felt such a strong connection with those monsters.

Slowly she undid the knot in her throat and said simply, still looking at the creatures in the room, "Were they ever real human kids?"

"Indeed. We used human babies. There is no other way to create a super human race, Captain. At least not now. But have solace in the possibility that perhaps even your own child is among these creatures. What a privilege! As I understand from your file, your child didn't die. She simply...went missing, didn't she, Captain?"

Captain Rodriguez's heart seemed to stop for what felt like an eternity. The possibility of her daughter having been transformed into such a heinous beast was so shocking and repulsive to her that a dark cloud seemed to build up abruptly over the Captain, raining rage down on her, drenching her in torrents of fury until she lashed out like a lightning bolt at the director, whom she could have killed with a single blow in that brief moment of seething wrath. But in keeping with their duty and training, two guards who were always close to the director intercepted her and took on the strikes meant for him.

"You won't get away with this!" Captain Rodriguez shouted violently from within the guards' tight grasps. They had to use all their combined strength just to contain her as she struggled to break free and lunge herself at the director to rip his heart out. "I will expose you. I will tell the world what you have done. You are finished at World Space Command. Finished!"

The director looked at Captain Rodriguez with intrigue. He emanated a low-sounding growl, which eventually she identified as the most macabre form of laughter. Fitting for such an apparently evil man.

"Silly little girl. I *am* World Space Command! I built this entire organization. Nothing happens here without my review and consent. So, explain to me exactly how you plan to expose me?"

"As soon as I get out of here— "

"You're not going anywhere, Captain. You see, I'm not finished. Not at all. I'm just getting started. You, on the other hand… I'm afraid your time is up. Don't say I didn't warn you. I offered you the way out. But you insisted on knowing the whole story. Now you know. Now you die," said the director pausing momentarily to gauge the Captain's stress level. She was solid as steel; her gaze fixed on him as if held there by an unrelenting magnet.

For his part, at least on the surface, the doctor appeared somewhat amused by the woman's resolute and rebellious spirit. It wasn't clear to anyone there if he was at all unnerved at a deeper level by this woman's demonstration of unbreakable will and mental fortitude. The director always seemed to have some secret knowledge about others, which usually gave him the upper hand in his dealings with everyone who opposed him. Everyone, that is, except Captain Rodriguez.

Doctor Martin gave her a quick smirk, as people do when crossing paths with casual acquaintances and acknowledging them. He continued saying, "And by the way, that story about your child being among the genetically enhanced, I wouldn't worry about it, Captain. I'm sure she wasn't recruited for the job. She must have ended up in some filthy brothel in some third-world country serving a purpose much more suited to her lineage."

He stepped back and motioned with a tilt of his head for the two men to drag the Captain by her arms closer to the entrance to the room. A third guard approached the door. Through the large window she could see the creatures still lying on the floor and the other two rummaging across the room. The director motioned at the man next to the door, who obediently pulled out a small hand-held device.

"Lieutenant," said the director, addressing the guard sarcastically, "our guests must be starving. After all, we've only served them one appetizer. It's dinner time," he eyed Captain Rodriguez maliciously as he spoke.

The guard pressed a button on his device and the nets subduing the rest of the creatures automatically retracted, freeing them. With a quick glance, the director instructed the men holding Captain Rodriguez to open the door and shove her in with those monsters. They pushed her so hard that she went tumbling forward, landing at one of those creature's feet. The beast grimaced at her as he stood over the Captain snarling and hissing. The others joined in surrounding the Captain. They squeezed together tightly until they were shoulder to shoulder, completely closing the spaces between them and any possible escape route.

The Captain peered at the monsters approaching her. She shifted around on the floor trying to anticipate the first attack in the hopes of thwarting it even though, deep down, she knew she would not stand a chance. But the attack never came. The creatures just stood there growling, hissing, and baring their teeth at her. Captain Rodriguez slowly began to rise to her feet keeping a close eye on the beings surrounding her. They remained static in their stances. Only their eyeballs followed her up as she finally stood tall within their circle. Quite unexpectedly, the creatures began to quiet down and hide their teeth. They raised their hands in her direction as children reaching out to a parent for comfort. They began to waddle toward the Captain and by the time they all managed to throw their arms around her, they had transformed back into the normal-looking human children she had rescued from Mars as they stood there hugging her tightly. The Captain was overwhelmed with a strange series of emotions similar to what she had experienced when she first encountered the

Martian children.

As if immersed in an elaborate dream, Captain Rodriguez was struck with a flood of images that streaked across her mind's eye as if they were all parts of a movie going fast forward on a screen. She found herself participant of a shared consciousness both human and other-worldly. An ethereal and elusive voice told her through those images and through plain, unspoken knowing that many other people from Earth had visited Mars aside from the original colonists. In fact, the Martian colony had long ago been established in secret. The original explorers had made a major find which answered conclusively the question: Are humans alone in the universe? The answer was no.

Deep within a cave, the first explorers had uncovered what initially appeared to be a ceramic statue of near human proportions. However, some of the characteristics of the sculpture seemed quite alien with an elongated cranium, extended appendages, an exceedingly thin torso, long neck, a small mouth with no lips, and extraordinarily large eyes seemingly sculpted shut. It was during transport that the explorers accidentally dropped the apparent sculpture, which led to a fracture that uncovered a hidden inner core of organic matter. In fact, the finding was no sculpture at all, but the encapsulated remains of a once living creature.

This finding, though it was never disclosed to the public, changed the entire approach to space exploration. It led directly to World Space Command's initiative to join efforts with several world government and non-government agencies, including NASA in the U.S., to form their official Mars Mission and Colonization project. Of course, by then they had already had their colony well established in secrecy. But they calculated that making it public would boost their revenue which would enable them to keep financing their secret efforts into the reanimation of Martian life by cloning the DNA from the sample they had found. The move proved to be wildly successful as funds poured in. This enabled World Space Command to expand the ambitions of its secret project while maintaining a proper supply of scientific discovery to satiate the public's and sponsor's demand for results in Martian research efforts.

For many years they attempted unsuccessfully to reproduce that alien life through its own means. Then they began to engage in animal/alien hybridization trials, which were also to no avail. There simply did not seem to be any animal on Earth compatible with the alien DNA. But that did not stop World Space Command; that is, Dr. Damian Martin. He first approached the top contributors and representatives from the different world governments and entities disclosing to them a cockamamie project to begin terraforming Mars for a speedier colonization. No one wanted to sign off on an expansion of the Mars Mission. That is to say, no one wanted to open their pocket books wider than they already had. This short-sightedness, in his view, only served to push the Doctor further away from humanity. But it was not the final straw.

The original human explorers and subsequent scientists and engineers who followed in the establishment of the

Martian base that Captain Rodriguez would visit many years later, frequently succumbed to some form of homesickness, radiation overexposure, or cabin fever. Dr. Martin saw this as an insurmountable flaw in the idea of human colonization of the planet. He concluded that humanity itself was just not suited in any way to inhabit any other place in the universe other than Earth. Therefore, the need to find the solution to this limitation was clear. And the Martian specimen offered that solution. Using human DNA as the base, he could create a hybrid specimen that in time would be perfected and turned completely into a new species.

But the plan was not without its problems, too. It seemed that the creatures that eventually resulted from the experimentations were, at first, completely deformed and unstable. Then, when they managed to stabilize the hybrid mixture, the resulting prototypes were prone to group infighting. Especially, if given the time to reach maturity without some strict program of cohesion. Therein lay another flaw. The hybrid creatures tended to bond to a single leader who could guide them into maturity as a whole. These were in short supply.

At the Martian colony one exceptional leader rose to the challenge. Her name was Amanda Ramses. She was a leading behavioral scientist and zoologist who had excelled in raising several alien-human hybrids into maturity. That is, until the day she refused to continue the work expected of her. Before World Space Command could have her transferred back to Earth, she took it upon herself to free all the creatures she had helped raise. The results were catastrophic. The creatures attacked several of her colleagues with mortal consequences, having interpreted her actions as a greenlight for an offensive.

Realizing that she had single-handedly sentenced the entire colony to a certain death at the hands of her hybrid troops, Amanda attempted to reverse her actions and have the creatures go back to their respective holding quarters. But before she could get a hold of the situation, a desperate and resentful fellow colonist found her unguarded and shot her dead. He, along with the remaining scientists and

other personnel were, thereafter, hunted
down slowly, one by one, during a period of
several months until there was no one left
but one man, the bewildered colonist whom
Captain Rodriguez would encounter when she
was on her search and rescue mission to the
Martian base: Dr. Edgar J. Ruby.

After that brief mental flight receiving the massive
download of information telepathically while in the
embrace of the Martian creatures, the Captain regained
awareness of her surroundings, realizing that she was still
at the World Space Command holding block. She felt her
head whirling as she struggled to process all of the data
spanning decades of experiences and perspectives from
different people, as well as aliens and hybrid beings. It
seemed as if time had stopped, but now she was finally able
to gather herself, turning her eyes to the glass wall.
Through it she saw Dr. Martin again. He and his men had
remained standing there witnessing the scene, watching
how those creatures—now turned into harmless children—
clung to her. As she stared at him, the director could see the
children lifting their heads as well and twisting themselves
around to aim their glowing red eyes at him. From
overhead Captain Rodriguez again heard that rumbling,
cryptic voice which characterized the doctor.

"How very brave of you, Captain. Impressive. But,
then again, that is precisely why I chose you to lead this

mission. You did not disappoint. You have felt how they connected with you so powerfully. Like mother and children. They are tied to you, Captain. And you will help me care for my...*our*...children until they are ready to fulfill their destiny."

"What makes you think I would ever help you further destroy these poor things? You're out of your mind. You can keep me prisoner, or you can kill me. But you will never force me to work for you."

"I beg to differ, Ana. You don't mind if I call you Ana, do you? Since we are going to be so much more intimately connected, I feel we should be more personable with each other."

"Go to hell, you monster!"

"Oh, please, Ana. Call me Damian. And by the way, that cannot be the manner in which we treat each other now that we are family, don't you agree?" The director took one step back and motioned someone over. A young girl stepped into the frame and stood next to him facing the window. Captain Rodriguez felt like someone had punched her in the gut. She doubled over when she saw the little girl's face. Breathless at the sight before her she whispered a name:

"Virginia…"

"That's right, Ana. It's your daughter," came the

director's menacing voice through the speaker. "Say hello to your mother, Virginia. You do recognize your mother, don't you?"

"Hello, mother," Virginia's voice sounded robotic, empty of affection.

"What have you done to her? She is not herself."

"Ana, please. I would never harm our little girl. She means so much to us. All my men feel like they are her uncles. It's the truth. Isn't that right, boys?" All the guards and personnel surrounding the director nodded and snorted an approval.

"We take good care of Virginia. And that is why you are going to return the favor and will take good care of our little litter of hybrids. You'll have supervised visits with Virginia but only if I see that you are fulfilling your duties as I assign them. Any small deviation from the path will result in dismissal of your visiting privileges. And if for some insane reason you should ever have the stupid idea of trying to escape I will catch you and you will pay… severely," he said turning his eyes on Virginia to drive home the point.

Captain Rodriguez gently moved aside two of the Martian children standing in her way and walked toward the window. The Martian's seemed perplexed and followed close behind her. As she reached the window she extended her hand at level with her daughter's face. Virginia simply looked past the Captain into space. With tears streaming from her eyes now she vowed silently that one day she would rescue her daughter and herself. Ana promised she would come back to kill the man who had taken her daughter from her. As if hearing her mental pledge, Dr. Martin interrupted her thoughts,

"It really isn't good to keep anything bottled up inside like that, Ana. I can practically read your mind. You would like nothing more than to hunt me down and kill me like a dog, wouldn't you? That's my girl. A decisive hunter!"

What had appeared simply as a wall in the room behind Captain Ana Rodriguez and the Martian young ones began to open like giant swinging doors revealing an exit leading directly to the open range outside the building. Captain Rodriguez was surprised and confused at the sight. Was he offering them freedom?

"Sorry, Captain. I'm afraid it is not exactly a way out so much as it is a way to give our Martians proper accommodations. We have acres and acres for miles on end of open space under the stars replete with prey to hunt. There is also a cabin awaiting you beyond those hills in the distance. That will be your home…that is, for as long as you need such a dwelling. I don't anticipate you will be making that your permanent home, though. For now, you will receive all further instructions, and your daughter's visits, there. Now go. Tomorrow is the start of a brand-new life…A brand new world."

Captain Rodriguez turned back to look at Virginia one more time. Dr. Martin placed his hand on Virginia's shoulder as if to remind the Captain of his power over her. She turned back around and began walking into the darkness defeated, her head hanging down. The Martian children followed in her footsteps like good little girls and boys walking in a straight line. Once outside, their eyes glowing red detected movement in the darkness causing their naked little bodies to begin shifting shape again readying for the hunt. As they achieved their transformation the Captain began to hear each of their voices not from their mouths but coming as thoughts directly into her mind. It was an endless barrage of unintelligible chatter streaming through with the occasional words and phrases she could actually make out.

"Join us," they said. "We missed you..."

Bewildered by this new ability to host other voices in her head, the Captain had no time to process the significance of these thoughts as she, too, began to experience a sudden physical urge to shed her skin, like a snake slithering across the ground, hidden in the shadows of the night. The chatter in her head grew louder and a strange thirst for blood overcame her senses. In the distance, she could not only hear but also smell the presence of a group of humans lost in the expanse; unwitting sacrificial victims whose fear was their most prominent signal attracting the now blood-thirsty Captain and her group of hybrid Martians ready to go on the prowl.

The Four Pioneers

One afternoon a child playing among the greenery of the colony's greenhouse spotted a lonesome figure out in the desert landscape fast approaching. When others were alerted they were bewildered at first believing it to be perhaps a true Martian alien lurking about. But soon they realized that the figure seemed to be wearing similar Martian colony gear. The first thoughts of it being their fallen comrade were dismissed. It would have been impossible for her to have survived. Her oxygen supply could not have lasted the entirety of her absence and still allow her the ability to make the trek back to base. But, miraculously, it was Olivia, their fallen comrade.

Once among her fellow colonists, Olivia told them of her tale of survival in what she believed—at first—to have been a dormant state, like hibernation. Something about her seemed strange, though. She appeared surprisingly relaxed and confident, as if she had not lived through a harrowing experience as they imagined she surely must have. The colonists were baffled by how she, in her cool, in-control demeanor contrasted clearly with them. They were accustomed to being a nervous breed of humans. Perhaps the uncertainty and scarcity of Mars had made them creatures filled with fears and angst because of the lack of insight into their own fates. As for her, it turned out that her tank had not retained the oxygen at all. Yet she was calm and composed. Olivia explained:

"My friends, I have been given a second chance at life. When I fell into that canyon I thought that I would surely die. But much to my surprise, when I awoke at the bottom, I found myself thinking that perhaps it had been the shock that had helped me remain numb to pain, for I felt none. As I thought about my life, I heard the slow but steady hiss of the tank which I thought would surely seal my fate. But when the hissing faded away I still breathed. Moments passed, not long it seemed. However, when I finally got up, I realized it had not been moments but days that had gone by. I could tell because I observed that the course of the sun on the horizon had shifted ever so slightly."

The crowd was astonished by the circumstances of their fellow colonist's miraculous tale. Some of them, however, seemed more agitated and skeptical of the proposition that one could survive such an ordeal.

"You mean you noticed the course of the sun changing on the horizon? Strange...I've never known you to be the avid naturist able to survive the outdoors guided by the movements of the heavens." questioned an onlooker named Carlos, one of the men who had accompanied Olivia on that expedition when she was thought to have been lost forever.

"I, too, felt perplexed and incredulous of my sudden abilities," the survivor responded with a minor edge of irritation. "It was then that I determined to make my way back to base."

"How *did* you make it back without navigation instruments? Clearly your suit had no power and you had no vehicle to rely on," questioned yet another colonist.

"It felt like simple intuition at first. Or perhaps that the fall had awakened hidden talents in me. As it turns out, it has. In fact, the fall freed me from that which kept me—has kept us all—from achieving our full potential... those oxygen tanks. Our whole oxygen production system. It must be tainted somehow. As it is, the Martian atmosphere itself is not as we had been told. It's full of breathable air! When I was walking back home free of the oxygen tank I could feel myself becoming so much more keenly aware of myself and my surroundings. It felt as if I had woken up after a deep sleep and suddenly I was more alert and aware of things that had been hidden from me. Many mysteries which I explored before and could not understand, now are revealed to me by my own inner processes. I think we have been kept in a dulled state of mind by these tanks."

"She must still be delusional from the fall," said a middle-aged woman as she pressed her way through the crowd. She continued,

"Right now, you need to rest and recuperate, honey. You'll feel better. Then we can figure out how you survived out there. Perhaps it was a miracle. God is great. He was looking out for you,"

Feeling awkward and patronized by the older woman's maternal response to the situation, she replied,

"I assure you it was not God's doing. I can prove to

37

you that what I am saying is true. The oxygen in these facilities has kept us stunted."

"This is ridiculous. We are oxygen-breathing creatures. Always have been, always will be. You've lost your mind. Out there you got nothing but Carbon dioxide. There is a much simpler explanation to why and how you survived. It certainly does not negate the need for breathable air. Do you expect us to turn off our oxygen production and simply walk out onto the Martian environment?" the middle-aged woman urged.

"Yes, that is precisely what I am recommending."

"No one is doing any such thing," said the colony spokeswoman. She was a mature lady named Carmen. Short, pudgy, pink, round cheeks and graying, curly hair falling just below her ears—Carmen projected authority that was open and democratic. She looked at Olivia directly, analyzing her from head to toe. Carmen continued,

"You said you can prove your claim. How?"

"I know where to find the evidence to corroborate my insight."

"Where would that be?"

"All I know is that the First Four left something behind which could allow this mystery to unravel. I believe somehow my survival out there in the Martian atmosphere and my new abilities of insight are tied to them."

"That's absurd! Everyone knows that the first colonists returned to Earth some time back. And besides, we have no way of contacting Earth, so how do you plan to communicate with them?" said a man in the crowd.

"We must either find what they left behind or find a way to get a hold of them and ask them directly," responded Olivia nonchalantly.

"Perhaps it would be convenient for you to return to your quarters and rest. You seem to be losing more and more contact with reality. Don't you remember? The Earth channel has been cut off for who knows how long," the man continued to poke at Olivia.

"Listen to me. I know it sounds crazy," she responded. "...but we can find what the First Four left for us here on Mars."

"We all were present when they boarded that ship and returned home. We saw it with our own eyes! They never said anything about additional contingencies other than what we know of here at base," said yet another male voice.

"Really? Tell me something, how long ago do you think that took place? Their departure, that is," Olivia asked, her eyes peering at the man.

"I don't know. I haven't been keeping a timeline of events. Haven't really paid mind to the passage of time, come to think of it. But I know it had to have been at least two years ago," Carmen responded although the question had not been directed at her.

"Two years? Try seventy years. You are not the only one who had not been keeping track of the date. We have all been oblivious to the passage of time. But once I was freed from the oxygen tank I was able to recover knowledge that has been apparently collecting in the back of my mind, like an internal, subconscious inner working...a backlog of sorts. So, seventy years since they left, plus the thirty since we all arrived, that makes one hundred years! We have been on this planet for one hundred years now and none of us were aware of more than the first thirty."

"You mean Earth years?" A voice in the crowd asked.

"Mars years..." Olivia responded without hesitation.

When the crowd heard what she had said, she didn't get a chance to finish speaking as her voice was drowned out by a sonorous laughter. Carmen looked her over again. She was tempted to dismiss Olivia's claims without consideration. But something stopped her. A voice in the back of Carmen's own mind wanted to scream, to yell, to break free and tell her that what Olivia was saying was true. That she needed to act fast.

Seeing that their leader grew silent at that seemingly absurd idea, some of the crew began to express concern about the nature of that conversation which appeared to be swaying Carmen in Olivia's favor.

"There is no way that we have just been going through the motions like sleep walkers for a whole century —Martian or otherwise. We are not zombies!" said Carlos, He continued,

"Carmen, you must be careful. The fate of the entire colony is in your hands. Olivia has been exposed to Mars in ways that none of us have ever been. It's possible that the reason she seems to have survived is due to an infection by some microbe that has turned her into a zombie. I mean, who knows, right? Maybe she wants to bite us and get us infected too!"

"That's enough of that. I will not have us all turn into some angry mob ready to lynch one of our own," said Carmen.

"Wait a minute. You're not saying you actually believe her, are you? Have you lost your mind as well? None of us would be here today if one hundred years had gone by. We'd all be worm food by now. Worse than that —dust. C'mon!" shouted Carlos throwing his arms in the air in apparent frustration.

"Hey! Don't forget who you are talking to. Carmen is still our elected leader," said one lady who had been providing beverages and some first aid to Olivia as they probed her for answers.

Olivia for her part simply looked at the woman with a warm regard, thanking her with a nod for her assistance in patching up a few scratches, but responded straightforwardly to those challenging her account,

41

"I simply made an observation based on a feeling about our experience here. When I was unconscious out there at the bottom of that canyon I saw many visions: people coming and going in ships from Earth, the passage of time based on the revolutions around the sun, the changes in some topographical features, and other things that I just cannot explain."

"So, what you're saying is that you could very well be entirely full of shit, am I right?" remarked Carlos disparagingly.

"That's enough! There is one very clear question here that has not been properly answered, and that is how did she manage to survive without the oxygen tanks? All else can be explained away by theorizing all night long, but it won't get us anywhere. So, let's focus on that clear mystery that seems to elude us." Carmen turned to Olivia and continued, "Okay, Olivia. Tell us how exactly is oxygen supposed to be bad for us?"

"I am not sure about the specifics. But what I can tell you is that I just know it is, and I can prove it. You have to trust me."

"Okay, then. You want a chance to prove it? Fine. Show us your proof," said Carmen sharply.

Olivia seemed to be taken by surprise. She paused and looked at Carmen briefly as if to decipher what she had heard. She finally replied saying,

"Gladly. I will need a small crew to travel—"

"Travel? Where? The Martian outdoors has kicked her butt plenty and she still want's more, ladies and gentlemen," shouted Carlos across the room throwing glances at random people in the crowd. Some acknowledged him with a chuckle. Others looked to Carmen for input, and she simply asked,

"Where would you need to go to accomplish that?"

"I know it may come as a huge surprise to everyone but there is a site far out in the western desert. We were not meant to know about it. But now that I have had this epiphany, I know where it is. I can't explain how I know. It's as if I have seen images of different people and places from a past life, and this place is one of them. I know it's there. It must hold the answers to all our questions."

"Sounds to me like you've known about this place all along." Carlos interjected skeptically. "Maybe you faked your little accident out there so we would think you were dead and leave you to do whatever it is you did out there!"

Olivia looked over at Carmen as if to ask her to at least be given the benefit of the doubt. Carmen, for her part, was torn between her practical sense which told her that Olivia's story seemed fantastical at best, and wholly delusional at worst. But there was also still a small part of her that told her she should indulge this claim and see where it would lead.

Olivia interrupted the silence of thinking with a

sense of urgency, "We must go now. There may be sandstorms headed our way. We cannot afford to be trapped midway there. I need a team of three volunteers."

"Very well. We shall uncover the merits of your claim. I am going with you. I need to see this for myself," Carmen responded. She looked around at the rest of the colonists and stated,

"Friends and colleagues, I can see you all are anxious to get to the bottom of this, as I am. Olivia's unbelievable survival and return from what all of us considered to have been her end raises many serious questions about our colony and our very existence. Rest assured that we will get the answers we need. I will go with Olivia and two others. The rest of you will carry out the work that must be done as always and await our return. Our crop is bountiful. Our families are healthy and strong. Little by little we increase our fuel reserves to the point that soon we could launch a trip back home as soon as we make contact with Earth again. If Olivia's claim that there is another site out there is true, this might be that opportunity we had been waiting for to get assistance from the homeland. There is nothing to fear. Return to your posts. Enjoy the pleasures of our gardens and each other's company. We will be back soon."

Hearing this, the rest of the colonists looked to one another as if searching for answers to unvoiced concerns. There was a heavy sense of incredulity in the air. Carmen simply moved on, pulling aside two of her officers saying,

"Carlos and Emanuel, you two will go with us,

since you have worked together before and know the terrain better than most. We will count on your capable expertise."

Carlos and Emanuel looked at each other speechless, almost doubting that their expertise really called for such a vote of confidence. But if they did feel apprehensive and unfit for the challenge, they kept it to themselves. They stood at attention, saluting their leader as soldiers would on Earth when in the presence of their Commander in Chief. Carlos, however, did have some concerns he wished to express to Carmen privately. He approached her and took advantage of the fact that Olivia had become distracted and in a low voice he whispered into Carmen's ear:

"Are you sure about this? How can we be certain her account is valid?"

Carmen looked at him earnestly and replied, "I just want to make sure we find out if there is anything out there we didn't know of. And, if there is, why weren't we briefed on it? You know, it occurs to me that maybe she is telling the truth. She was lost out there for quite some time. She may have come across something that none of us in the colony can account for. I'd say that's worth investigating." She nodded and peered at him through raised eyebrows as if seeking his acknowledgement.

"That's exactly what I'm saying! What if this whole thing is a set up? I saw this woman take a dive into that canyon that no human I know could have survived," Carlos stated seemingly incapable of being persuaded.

She knew Carlos had a point, but still something compelled her to give Olivia a small benefit of the doubt. Perhaps it was her inner angel which always held out the possibility that miracles can happen. Or maybe just that, as a scientist, she knew that in this case the simpler explanation wasn't that Olivia had had her body snatched by Martians, but that there was some real-world reason for her survival that did not involve other-worldly intervention, either in a physical or spiritual sense.

Carmen knew she had to simmer things down in order to get things done. Employing her natural charm and skill at de-escalation, which was her trademark as their elected speaker, Carmen stepped in closer to him as she continued saying with a slight hint of humor, "Why don't you just go ahead and tell her you like her and get it over with? This push and pull is getting to be a little ridiculous." She gave Carlos a wink and a sly smile as she padded him on the shoulder.

Carlos took a step back feigning offense. He held back a smirk and shifted his gaze slowly from Carmen to Olivia blurting out loud as if still suspicious of her,

"What's the rush to go out there? People have always talked about sandstorms but none of us have ever seen one. By the way, how do you even know there'll be a storm? You got a doppler radar for a brain now?"

"I never said that there was a sandstorm coming. I said there could be one, so we should move fast before we get held back in one. There is no time to waste. Especially not on petty differences," Olivia retorted defiantly squaring off face to face with Carlos. "But if you have a problem with me maybe we can step outside and resolve it, sandstorm or no sandstorm,"

"Ouch! Touchy, touchy. Is that a challenge? How cute. Should I wear an oxygen mask? Oh, wait, that's right. No need for masks. After all its Mars out there, people!" Carlos laughed as he looked around, as always, for supporters among the faces in the crowd. And as always, a couple of men (chief among them, his right-hand man, Emanuel) laughed along with him.

"You can go ahead and just put a chloroform-filled rag over your ugly face and take yourself out, for all I care," said Olivia, still staring him down.

"Oh, yeah? Well, why don't you just bite me, zombie lady!"

"Alright, that is enough with you two! We will get nothing done with both of you fighting like grade-school kids. Solve your problems on your own time. This mission involves the interests of the entire colony and I will not let your bickering get in the way of the mission. Is that understood? Now let's get going," Carmen ordered, piercing their eyes.

The crew of four embarked on their trip beyond the western reaches of the colony. They found themselves farther than any of them had ever been. After some time, they began to wonder whether they had been wise in following along on what felt increasingly like a wild goose chase on the barren Martian landscape. It was Carmen who felt particularly duped. Surely no one had made the trip way out there, not even the First Four.

She was about to call off the search in spite of Olivia's assurances that they would find what they were looking for. Then someone noticed a faint outline in the distance. It could have been a huge rock or some other part of the landscape but the sharp edge, barely visible with their rover's light amid the darkness and the dust swirling around, gave Carmen reason to instruct Carlos to keep going until they reached the structure. It was a square-shaped facility easily identifiable as property of the Mars Four Corporation. They noticed a docking port and rode all the way up to it where they were able to dock their vehicle automatically, as a censor picked up the company vehicle's signature allowing them to enter without having to don their suits. Just to put on one of those things took them at least an extra ten minutes to mount and secure. To Olivia it all made no difference because she was certain that they did not need oxygen suits at all.

Once inside, the crew did not know what to expect. The facility lacked many of the implements that were so customary to them for daily operations on their base. It was clear that this facility was not at all intended for daily operations and living quarters. There was a faint hum coming from the walls of the building. It was bewildering that this place had seemingly been unoccupied for an untold number of years as evidenced by the significant accumulation of dust on surfaces and yet there seemed to still be mechanisms maintaining a proper climate control and other processes working within that enclosure. The crew flashed their lights on the walls looking for buttons, switches, and touch surfaces. Carlos was the first to find a dimly lit pad glowing red on a wall. As he wiped the layer of dust off the surface of the screen, the lights in the interior of that facility turned on, engulfing them in a bright, fluorescent light tinged with a blueish hue.

In the middle of the room Olivia saw something that looked like a podium. It had a panel with dimly lit green touch-screen buttons. One button read "Extract Capsules." Olivia did not wait for the others' input and simply pressed on the screen. They could hear a mechanical sound rumbling directly below them. The floor started to shift and vibrate. The crew managed to jump off just as the moving parts broke open, revealing four egg-shaped capsules the size of coffins emerging from the ground.

Olivia and Carmen walked around the capsules looking for something to indicate their use. Carlos came around in the far end and began his own inspection. Upon seeing his partner move in for a better look, Emanuel followed suit circling around the capsules until he reached the narrower end opposite his companion. Once there Emanuel noticed another touch screen light up. But instead of pressing buttons to see what would happen he motioned Carlos over to take a look. Carlos moved closer to see what his partner had found and instantly knew that it was the answer to the question they all had in mind.

"I think I know what these are".

"What's that?" asked Carmen.

"Cryogenic hibernation capsules," Carlos responded without taking his eyes off the capsules.

"But why would Mars Four have them installed here in secret?" Carmen voiced the question talking to herself mostly. "I thought they only used these things for space travel. What would a hibernation facility be doing out here in the middle of nowhere?"

"I don't think we were meant to know about them.," proposed Olivia in her newly acquired matter-of-fact expression.

Carmen considered that momentarily and questioned, "But then how was it that it was revealed to you?"

"I guess there's only one way to find out...We ask the sleepers," said Carlos. He went ahead and pressed a button on the surface that said "Retrieve".

A series of hissing and slushing sounds ensued, followed by a transformation as the lid popped up and split in half with each part sliding off to either side. The crew could now see clearly inside the capsules. There, under a thin, clear veil in the capsules were four individuals; two men and two women. Carlos proceeded to press another button at the feet of the capsules that read "Reanimate." After engaging the reanimation sequence for two of the capsules the crew noticed that the individuals began to convulse as their thin veil retracted and exposed them while the liquid that had held them submerged dissipated into the interior of the capsule below their bodies. Olivia immediately understood what was happening and lunged at Carlos to prevent him from reanimating the other two.

"Wait!" she yelled. "You're killing them. Look at these two. They are obviously struggling to breathe."

As the convulsions resided, the couple did not seem to be breathing at all. Carmen looked at the men and said,

"Quick, help me give them CPR!" She began by providing the chest compressions. She turned to Emanuel and said, "You get over here. Carlos help Olivia. Hurry!"

Carlos rushed to assist Olivia. But no matter how well-trained they were in those techniques, they were unable to revive them. They watched the pair just lay there motionless, unable to breath. The crew looked at each other and then all eyes fell on Carlos.

"What? How was I supposed to know?" he shouted defensively.

"We must always evaluate the situation before moving forward on anything. One wrong step on this planet could lead to catastrophe. Everyone knows that!" Olivia shouted furiously.

"I never intended for this to happen. It was a simple mistake. Get the hell off my back! You think you're so goddamn perfect? This wouldn't have happened if it hadn't been for you bringing us out here to begin with. We were doing quite fine at base living our lives, doing our jobs. You want to talk about catastrophes? How about your little plan to get us all to ditch our oxygen tanks? You're out of your goddamn mind!"

"I'm smart enough to know that I don't know how long these people have been down there and that there must be some procedure to reanimate them in a safe manner. Perhaps something with instructions...like this!" Olivia pulled out a tablet which seemed to pop out at that opportune moment from a receptacle underneath one of the capsules. Indeed, it was a list of steps for reanimation. Had they followed that guide beforehand, they could have avoided the deaths of their suspended companions.

"Alright, enough of that. We gain nothing by pointing fingers. What do we do now, Olivia?" Carmen asked.

Olivia headed to the touch screen on each capsule and pressed the button to submerge the dead back into a cryonic state.

"First of all," Olivia said after seeing the two capsules return to their underground cavities, "...we should leave them in there. Since rigor mortis has not set in, it is possible to retrieve them at a later date and attempt resuscitation with the proper instruments. In the meantime, we should transport the other two back to base and reanimate them properly."

"We'll go suit up and come around the front to extract the capsules and load them on the transport. You'll need to open the door for us from the inside," said Carlos looking at Carmen. He was intentionally avoiding looking at Olivia directly. He turned to Emanuel and motioned with his head for him to follow. Emanuel joined up with Carlos headed to the vehicle.

Three days later, as the initial fanfare had died down and the rest of the colonists had returned to their duties having lost interest in the sleepers, those attending them noticed that the male had begun to move. They called Carmen over to witness the awakening. Carmen convened the rest of the crew that had assisted her in recovering the pair. Only after the man opened his eyes did the attendee press the button that would remove the thin veil and allow him to breathe the air outside of his cocoon. The man appeared disoriented and confused.

"Where am I?" he asked.

"You're at the Mars Four colony. Can you tell us your name?" said Carmen.

He had to think for a few moments and then replied, "I am…Benjamin."

"We are having a little trouble understanding how it is that you and your partner ended up in these hibernation capsules," Carmen motioned with her hand at his and his companion's capsules, which Benjamin looked at as if completely oblivious as to who could be in it. She continued "…Nobody mentioned you to us. Can you give us answers to these questions?"

"Who is in there?" he asked looking over at the other capsule.

"There is a young woman in that one. We have no clue who she is. We don't even know who you are. Tell us about yourself. How did you two end up in the cryogenic facility? Who put you there? Do you know how long ago this happened?" Carmen pressed him for answers. Benjamin, however, had his own set of questions before he answered anything.

"The others...two...another man and woman. Where are they?"

"First things first, Benjamin. The others remained in the cryogenic facility. We need you to tell us what's going on."

"What's going on? I don't know what's going on. What year is it?" he responded still in a state of confusion.

"Year?" Carmen repeated the question with a puzzled look on her face, as if she had never been asked that.

"It is the year 100 to be exact...in the Martian year-count, that is," Olivia intervened with her increasingly confident stance as to the actual passage of time that no one else had seemed to notice.

"My god. That would make it roughly 2225 A.D. on Earth. What's happened? Did someone finally contact Mars Four command center?" asked Benjamin.

"Nah, E.T. never phoned home," added Carlos

54

sardonically. He had been observing the interaction impatiently from the sidelines.

"We're not sure how long it's been, Benjamin. Olivia here claims that she has had a revelation and that, apparently, the Mars colony is truly a full century old. But it might just be the crazy ranting of someone who, herself, just came out of a suspended animation period; although a much shorter one. The reality is that we do not know. That is why we need you to tell us more about yourself. What happened? Why did you all end up submerged?" Carmen asked him the same questions patiently, sitting on a chair next to his capsule. The rest of the crew stood watching.

"It's not wrong, that theory of yours," said Benjamin looking at Olivia now.

"What do you mean she is not wrong?" Carlos intercepted before Olivia could respond.

By this time Benjamin seemed to be easing into himself, fully regaining his wits.

"Let me begin by answering your first questions…"

"Yes, why don't you do that?" retorted Carlos getting increasingly jumpy, suspecting that they were being duped by this guy as he took his time to fess up.

Benjamin was visibly taken aback at his outburst. The others all glanced over at Carlos momentarily as if to ask him for courtesy then returned their expectant gazes back to Benjamin.

"We were supposed to have only been suspended for about a year. There were problems on Earth that were increasingly getting in the way of Mars Four's missions. International disputes, terrorism, war. The last I remember before we went under is that there was another nuclear standoff between the superpowers. I don't know what happened, but if your assessment is correct and it has been as long as you say, I am guessing nothing good came of it. But you all probably already know all about that."

He extended his arm, reaching out to signal at Olivia to grab the tablet for him and hand it over. She was initially unaware of his gesture but then she noticed him trying to point with his chin as he spoke. She finally understood and handed it to him from a small table next to his capsule. Benjamin continued speaking as he took the tablet in his hands and began swiping across its surface scrolling through several displays on the device.

"Initially, we were told that we would be reanimated when things cooled down and, in the meantime, they would use our servants to continue our work…"

He paused briefly then continued saying, "Ah, yes. Here it is. The Mars Clock record indicates how long we have been submerged. It is as you said, Olivia." Benjamin handed her the tablet for her to witness the proof and pass around.

"You mean it truly has been decades?" asked Carlos with a troubled look on his face.

"Indeed. That tracker doesn't lie," responded Benjamin almost proudly.

Carmen redirected the conversation back to something that had caught her attention. "You said something about the use of servants..." She seemed to struggle with both the idea that more than three times as many years had transpired than she knew of, which they had lived in a state of inertia, and with the idea that the First Four had held 'servants,' which was difficult to accept.

"Well, yes. Don't all colonists have them? Surely you all were provided a helping crew, weren't you?"

By the way they looked at him, Benjamin could tell they knew nothing of what he was talking about.

"Our servants...or assistants...were simple-minded half-breeds created combining mechanical and organic parts at first," continued Benjamin. "The result was an android that could eat, sleep, and breathe just like us, humans. But after initial trials apparently, they found that these androids began 'dying' prematurely. Nobody understood why. Then someone on Earth had a brilliant idea. They determined that, since these beings were partly organic and shared a mental capacity that could almost always outmatch human consciousness and wit, maybe the problem was that they were dying because of a lack of purpose; an underlying imperative for survival aside from self-serving goals...a sense of community.

"So, they began embedding human thought

structure and memories into these androids to give them a sense of belonging to something bigger, and therefore, a reason to live. But they soon found that these androids indeed exceeded human ingenuity and physical ability, and even existential longevity. Placed under the right circumstances, they wouldn't even age. This would be a problem to colonists and Earth communities alike. I guess they didn't want to risk having this new creature get to a point that it could eclipse the human race. So, they modified their internal makeup to behave more like microaerophiles.

"Now, if you know your microorganisms—which I really don't, but this is what I was told by the delivery crews—you know that microaerophiles suffer under high levels of oxygen. Some of them actually require elevated levels of carbon dioxide to thrive. And what is the Martian atmosphere composed of? You guessed it, CO_2, my friends. In essence, this was a win-win scenario. What better place to send these new creations than to Mars, where, if they were to run out of oxygen, or there happened to be irreparable system failures these creatures would still thrive, even if humans didn't make it."

"But if an organism thrives under elevated levels of CO_2 and yet lives in an environment of decreased CO_2 and elevated Oxygen, such as in the Mars colony, wouldn't that kill that organism?" asked Carmen.

"You are correct. However, if you equilibrate the environment to include just enough CO_2 to allow these beings to exist yet include oxygen to partly oxidize them from the inside, you get the perfect slave. Able to work

58

with a goal in mind and a shared sense of purpose, for she or he is part of a greater community, the human community. But at the same time stunted in their capacity to think and process information. Their brains were essentially programed to work at 10% capacity—human capacity, that is."

By this point the crew could not avoid looking over at one another puzzled by what they heard. It seemed that this man's answers were creating more problems than they solved.

"What was your role in all of this?" asked Carmen.

"Oh, I was simply one of the original four colonists. We had no clue what the Mars Four Corporation had in mind when they sent us out here. They had told us it was for humanity to simply establish the first foothold until further developments could enable the full-scale settlement of the planet. We thought we were just going to live the rest of our lives here and die alone. But after the first year, seeing that the colony was struggling quite a bit, the first wave of ships began arriving bringing more supplies, equipment, facilities, and what at first we thought were other people. It turned out to be those newly created androids...

"They told us that these crossbred beings were here to establish the first planet-warming facilities that could in time terraform this planet into one resembling Earth's oxygen-rich atmosphere. But then the wars began back home. It all became quite dire. They ordered us into these capsules to await further human-led missions after things cooled off. They wanted to ensure our survival so we could assist the other arrivals, since we had spent a few years here already. The only way to make sure of that was to submerge us until the missions could resume."

"Wait a minute. What are you saying? Are you hearing this, Carlos? I mean, Jesus, what is this guy talking about? Why did Mars Four Corporation only set up capsules for you guys? What about the rest of us?" Emanuel was finally breaking his silence with this piercing interrogation.

"Oh my God…" said Benjamin staring intently at Emanuel as if he had just made an astonishing discovery.

"What are you looking at?! Stop staring at me like I'm some kind of freak! If anything, you're the freak!" shouted Emanuel.

"No. You're not a freak. You weren't even sent here by Mars Four command to extract us, were you?"

Olivia stepped in before anyone could respond saying, "No. We were not. I brought them here after my odyssey out in the Martian desert alone without oxygen."

"Which explains nothing and makes no sense," inserted Carlos as he turned his attention to Benjamin. "Neither of you are making any goddamn sense! Why were we left out of the loop about this facility? That's what I would like to know."

"I'll do you one better, my friend. Why do you

think that you look as young as you do even though you were not frozen in time like us? I bet you haven't aged more than a couple of years, even though it has been a full martian century since the colony was established. How do you explain that?"

"Are you saying that...we are these androids that you are talking about?"

"Yes. That is exactly what I am saying! My god, it must be that my mind is too foggy. I can't recall having seen any of your faces before the deep sleep. But, in any case, it all makes sense. That's why you all didn't know about the cryogenic facility. You weren't supposed to know."

"No. That's impossible! I have a family. I remember my childhood. You're not going to tell me that I'm some kind of machine. I'm a human being, damnit!" Emanuel shouted, horrified by such idea.

"I am sorry to say so but it is true. You *are* what I am saying you are. Think about it. When was the last time someone you know died? When was the last time someone was born? I'm sorry. I know this is hard for you to take in. However, I urge you to look at this in a more positive light. Look at me. Look at my partner in there," his head motioned toward the other capsule.

"We are so fragile and flawed. The universe doesn't belong to us. How could it? We've spent so many years working on this planet and wasting our time because of our inability to solve our major problems. So is this it? This is life on Mars? What's the difference? Earth or Mars it's all the same. We are still just as lost and confused as ever. We still don't know if there are any other forms of life other than what came from Earth. Humans are just as alone and afraid on Mars as they were on Earth.

"And what about God? Where is he? It turns out he's just as much of a mute out here as he was on Earth. We are no better off here. It's the same pathetic existence. You go to work, you come home. You eat, you shit, you find some mindless entertainment until your brain is dull, and only then you hit the sack until the next day when you have to get your ass back up and do it all over again. On, and on, and on like mice on an old wheel spinning aimlessly. And for what? To grow old and die and let the next batch of clueless bastards replace us and continue the same damn cycle into eternity. You know what would have happened here if we would have fully colonized this planet, don't you?" Benjamin asked rhetorically as he scanned the faces before him.

"The same stupid crap," he pressed on without waiting for a response, "that happened on Earth. That's what. We would have bunched up into gangs that wouldn't have been able to reconcile their differences, and then started an arms race until we got to the ultimate weapons that would have threatened not just our enemies but our own group as well. You see, it turns out it wasn't something about our existence on Earth that led us toward annihilation; it wasn't something in the water or in the air. It was us. It's always been us. There is no hope. We are doomed to fail. Unless we are able to transcend the human condition. In which case, if we wanted to ensure our legacy

62

among the cosmos the trick was not to find ways to send humans to inhabit other planets; the trick was to extract the essence of humanity and insert that into an adequate vehicle that could start over for us and perhaps achieve what we were never able to do: to live in peace and harmony and reach our full potential..."

He paused to look into an empty corner of the enclosure as if to collect his thoughts, then continued, "And that is why you are here, my friends. Now I truly see that the universe has its own plans and schemes. It used us in order to get you, and now here you are. Our time is over. When we die humanity will die...but its legacy will live on in every one of you. Perhaps one day we can all make a trip back to Earth and find your makers, if they survived, and maybe more of your kind, as well. But in one hundred years, you all have survived. You all have made it without killing yourselves or each other. That is success!"

"Success?" said Olivia pensively, "We never had the free will to choose otherwise to begin with. We've been living a complete farce."

"What should we do now?" Carmen asked him as if asking a great sage for worthy advice.

"Go tell your comrades the good news. Tell it on the mountains of Mars! Inhale deeply the Martian air and become what you were meant to be. The true Martian settlers. Put us back in the cryogenic underground because here among you we would only get in the way. Look for a file titled 'Project Progeny' on the Earth satellite link, if you can regain access to the portal. It will tell you all you

63

need to know about your kind. You'll find instructions as to the proper CO2/oxygen ratio for optimal performance of your…species. Remember, you will still require oxygen for survival, but at a significantly reduced rate. And you're wrong, Olivia. It was not a farce. It was the birth of your kind. Now you all will be free to go forth and live. In time you all will be able to extract and use this world's resources to produce the things you will require to multiply and conquer this planet and eventually the entire galaxy and beyond! Good luck, my friends. I hope you can accomplish the unity that humanity could never achieve. Oh, but we tried. God knows we tried."

The crew could hardly process what they had heard. Benjamin for his part appeared severely weakened and had laid back down into the capsule. After some time, they noticed he had fallen back into a deep sleep. Without consulting the others, Olivia stepped forward and initiated the submersion process.

Moments that seemed eternal elapsed. The crew appeared to be frozen in time. Someone eventually broke out of the spell and they all sprang into action as if they instinctively knew what needed to be done. Carlos and Emmanuel wheeled the capsules back onto the transport vehicle and soon they were all on their way back to the hibernation facility.

Along the way, no one had much to propose in the way of commentary. They were simply going to place the capsules back underground and head back. Carmen and Olivia did not truly need to be there, since Carlos and Emanuel were quite capable of making the delivery on their own, but it felt necessary anyway, so they accompanied the men. Perhaps they were each trying to understand more, learn more, think more. What would come next for the colony? They wrestled with that question. They looked at each other and knew they were pondering the same thing. When they got back to base there would have to be a soul-searching as to what direction to take.

The men had put Benjamin's capsule in place, but as they wheeled the second capsule into the building they heard a sound coming from inside. They stopped in their tracks, not sure if they had actually heard the sound or had imagined it. Everyone was silently waiting for another sign. When they heard another bang from within the capsule they knew the woman had awakened. They opened it and stood back. The woman had opened her eyes and seemed confused and lost. After a few minutes, she sat up and looked around, puzzled.

"Where am I?" she asked at random, trembling.

"We're on the Mars Four— "

"Mars Four?" she interrupted Carmen before she could finish. Carmen continued:

"What is your name?"

The woman looked at Carmen acknowledging the question, then looked down into the capsule as if pondering deeply, searching for a response.

"Linda... My name is Linda," she replied finally.

"Who are you people?"

"My name is Carmen, that is Carlos, she is Olivia, and over there is Emmanuel." The crew waved or said hello. Linda was a young woman of about 23 years of age. She was slim, had a long neck, high cheekbones, and long, straight, black hair. Carlos and Emanuel looked at each other as they marveled at her beauty. Linda mostly directed her gaze at Carmen since she had been the one taking command of the discussion and said,

"How long have I been suspended?"

"We don't really know. According to...some sources you all have been down there for seventy years." Carmen looked at Olivia as she said this. She turned back to Linda who had a puzzled look in her eyes.

"Seventy years? That can't be. These pods weren't designed for that kind of duration. Who was it in that capsule?"

"A man. Said his name is Benjamin."

"Benjamin? What else did he tell you all?"

"That we are cyborgs sent out here prefabricated to be the human's gophers on Mars," Carlos said making his opinion known clearly. "Apparently, in order to keep us from breaking out on our own, your buddy there said that we've been given a bad mix of oxygen that would keep us dulled...you know? Being that we are machines that run primarily on carbon dioxide and all...A bunch-a bullshit, if

66

you ask me." He looked at the rest of the crew. He looked at Olivia as if to refute her story again just to spite her.

"Cyborgs? Carbon dioxide?" Linda reflected, visibly amazed by the account. She suddenly broke into an uncontrollable laughter. The crew didn't know what to make of her outburst.

"Okay, you mind explaining just what the hell is so goddamn funny?" Carlos demanded. Carmen moved in closer to Linda as if to silently but visibly back Carlos' query, awaiting Linda's response.

"I'm sorry. Please excuse me. I don't mean to sound as if I am poking fun at any one of you. It's just that Benjamin is not the most reliable source by any measure. He's like our boy who cried wolf. Full of tall tales. You people aren't robots...not entirely, that is."

"Not entirely?" Emmanuel interjected forcefully. "What's the story with Benjamin? Is he crazy? And what exactly do you mean we are not entirely robots? No more delays, lady. We need to know the truth."

"All I meant about Benjamin is that maybe he was a bit disoriented and didn't know what he was talking about. The truth of the matter is that you all are not machines, although in a way you are taking part in a project designed by a computer program to test your problem-solving skills, to keep them sharp for when you arrive on Mars."

"What do you mean when we arrive? We are on Mars. We've been here for years, decades!" said Carlos adamantly, now seemingly siding on Olivia's argument about the passage of time.

"That is all part of the illusion. This entire facility is an illusion." By now Linda was speaking, not as one who has just risen from a decades'-long sleep, but as one who has just revealed an inside prank that was, by all measures, just not funny. She was visibly trying hard to contain a smirk that insisted on springing up on her face.

"Maybe you're the one who is confused," said Carlos. "You did just wake up from long nap there, sweetheart. Your brain must be foggy. Just a while ago you didn't even know where you were. Or were you leading us on?"

"I guess it's just that I like to take part in these exercises, too. As your virtual assistant, I am the only one who is fully aware of what is going on at all times, and it can get quite lonesome and boring around here. That is why I like to get fully into character and play the role. But that's all this is, a role-playing exercise. You all have been living in a simulation, nothing more than a dream. At this very moment, you are hurtling across space. You are on your third month of the voyage. Mars Four decided they needed to equip your trip with simulators for your mental health and viability, since you will remain suspended in deep sleep for the entire duration of the trip. They conducted studies that showed that when subjects were provided with plenty of guided dreams, they tended to coalesce a lot better as a group. This, they felt, could ensure a greater level of success, being that you all are on a very special mission to establish the first-ever human colony on Mars."

68

"So, this is all just a dream?" Emanuel asked in a deflated manner.

"Something like that. Like I said, this is a guided dream, a simulation for your subconscious, and I am your guide. I suppose the mission directors determined you all were better off not knowing about this program. I suppose they figured that, even though this is for your group's overall well-being, you all might not have been willing to agree to immerse yourselves in these exercises, given that you have absolutely no control over any aspect of the simulations."

Linda paused for a moment, touching her index finger to her lower lip and rolling her eyes up and to the left as if searching for something else to add to the discussion. As if nothing else came to mind, she simply threw her hands up in the air and concluded, "Unfortunately, this exercise has gone-on quite a while. It is beginning to affect your vitals. Which is why it must be terminated, although I was truly enjoying playing this role. A minor one, but you know what they say, 'There are no small roles.'"

"Prove it." shouted Carlos. "Show us that this is all a dream. I've had dreams all my life, lady. Usually when you find out you're just dreaming, that's when you wake the hell up. I ain't waking up yet! I guess you must be full of shit!"

Linda briefly looked at them as if considering something, then said,

"Ok, observe."

She pointed a device at Carlos which froze him instantly in place. The others did not notice at first what it was that she had intended by pointing that device, since no ray of light or projectile emerged from it. But soon they all realized that Carlos was clearly immobilized, as if he had become a statue with his boots glued to the floor. He didn't even appear to be breathing. Emanuel approached his friend and called out to him. Nothing. He got closer and touched Carlos on the shoulder and still he did not respond. Emanuel got in front of him to look him straight in the eyes and noticed they looked like lifeless glass beads. He then looked over to Linda who was smiling wickedly.

"Are you all satisfied?" she asked.

"So where is your proof?" said Carlos as he became unglued. He instantly noticed Emanuel standing right in front of him. He exclaimed, "Hey, whoa, what are you doing, man? You're right in my face!"

His companions looked at one another and then at Carlos.

"What?!" he nearly shouted.

"I think she might be telling the truth, Carlos. We might be just experiencing this artificially," Carmen informed him.

"Bullshit," he responded viscerally.

70

"Seriously, man. She pointed something at you and you froze right where you were," said Emanuel jumping in. "That's why I was standing in front of you like that. I was trying to talk to you but you wouldn't respond. It's like you didn't see me."

"It's time to say goodbye, folks," Linda stepped in. "You'll all be seeing each other in the next exercise. For now, you will simply go into a deeper sleep. Just darkness. A mental void. It will help you reboot your minds and shed any anguish from this simulation. I'll return for you after some time with a new challenge. Perhaps even a new adventure on a different planet. Or even on Earth itself. That would be fun, wouldn't it?" Linda asked as if she were a mother speaking warmly to her children. "You all can say goodbye, hug each other, or whatever you wish. But I must terminate this program, so please do it quickly."

The crew closed-in together and hugged one-another. While they were huddled they looked at one-another and an unspoken plan was hatched. Nobody trusted Linda's version of events. For all they knew she was either a sociopath, which would explain why she had been placed in the capsule. In Carlo's view, she was as crazy as Benjamin...and Olivia. He addressed the group in low voice, almost a hum,

"I'll tackle her and you go for the weapon," he said looking at Emanuel who nodded slightly, almost imperceptibly so as to not give himself away. As they broke formation, Linda pointed the device at Emanuel without warning and he fell to the ground, slowly fading away until he completely disappeared.

"Don't worry," Linda reassured them "there was no pain involved. None of you will feel any pain. I am simply doing this to entertain myself. This isn't truly necessary. I could simply 'pull-the-plug' as people say and this would cease immediately. But what's the fun in that, right?" she said with a chuckle.

The remaining crew looked nervously at each other. They did not appreciate Linda's apparent complete control of the situation. In an instant, they rushed her and pinned her down on the floor. Carlos held her down while Olivia and Carmen struggled to take the device from Linda's hand.

"You do realize that this is futile, don't you? None of this is actually happening. You all are simply dreaming!" Linda said, cackling through her breath.

"Quick," Carlos spoke up looking at Carmen, "take that thing and zap her!"

"I don't even know how this works. There is nothing on it. It looks like a plastic toy."

"Maybe she controls it with her mind," Carlos surmised.

"Well then go open her capsule. We'll put her in there and then figure out what to do," Olivia suggested.

"What about Emanuel?" Carmen remembered.

"Tell us where you sent Emanuel. How can we find him?" Carlos asked, looking at Linda as he tightened his hold on her legs and arms, mounting her.

"I've told you already. Emanuel is safe. Just like you are. Except he is soundly asleep. You all, on the other hand, are probably shifting and shuffling all around in your capsules," said Linda still attacked by laughter.

"What if it's true? What if this is all a dream?" Carmen asked her crew as she opened the capsule.

"You folks need to make up your minds soon. I am getting a reading on your vitals. It doesn't look good. Getting overly stressed while in stasis may produce too much toxicity in your systems leading to organ failure or worse. What'll it be?"

"You want to let her point that thing at you and make you disappear? Be my guest," Carlos shouted looking at Carmen then at Olivia. "I, for one, am not about to let this witch take me out like that. You think if she truly could kill this supposed simulation she wouldn't have done it by now? It's obviously a lie. She can't do shit. I'm putting her down. Then I'm getting in that vehicle and going back to base. Our mission has changed drastically. I say we make a clean break. We've got enough fuel to propel us far enough to be able to catch up with the orbiting Sling Blade. Hopefully, we can dock with it and initiate the rotation sequence to hurl us out toward Earth's vicinity. That should get us out far enough to be able to send some signal home from a clear vantage point. That's our only shot at getting back. It's obvious that whatever happened over there they are not going to come looking for us. It's up to us to rescue ourselves. Now who's with me?"

They managed to force Linda back into the capsule and submerge her into the ground. She kept banging against the interior of her confinement with all her might non-stop. Strangely, she also kept laughing so hard that the crew felt they could still hear her days later after they had returned to base. Nonetheless, they pressed forward and enacted their bold plan blasting out of the Martian atmosphere in an attempt to find the way back home.

From that point on, in the dark space between the red planet and Earth, the first four human Mars colonists (Carmen, the mission commander; Olivia, the medical specialist; and Carlos, and Emanuel, the technicians) continued to hurl across the cosmos inside their gyrating ships. From the point of view of one of the crew members, who happened to wake up mid-hibernation and stared into the dark enclosure of their ship past the looking glass of the hibernating capsule, there was no telling if they were coming or going. They would not know where they were headed until they landed.

Love in the Garden of Eden

...4,3,2,1 lift off! We have lift off of the spaceship Pioneer en route to Mars to pave the way for humanity's settlement of that planet as the first colony on an alien world...

Karina's heart rate was normal. She was a stone-cold adventurer. An eager explorer. She looked forward to that six-month trip to Mars as a time to meditate on the meaning of life, her life. Even if, as many on Earth speculated, she and her crew would probably die so far away from all the comforts and conveniences of the home planet—alone— she did not flinch. In her view, by going on this mission, she would be accomplishing more in the remaining few days, weeks, or months, if not years, on Mars than she had accomplished in the entire 29 years of her life on Earth. Even if that meant nothing more than simply being one of the first two women on the red planet. She was happy to be leaving that legacy behind for others to see.

In actuality, more than her desire to be a space explorer and Martian pioneer, what Karina wished to accomplish with this one-way trip was to completely sever the link to her past as one would cut off a gangrenous finger. Even as she sat there surrounded by so much advanced technology, surrounded by a group of companions from various places on Earth, all of them feeling so happy and excited about doing something that few people (but especially no girl from her country, much less her village) would ever dream of doing, she was still haunted by her past.

The ship began to shake violently while the thrusters roared as they propelled the massive ship off the ground. Karina could feel the vibrations on her body shifting her suit, which at first had seemed to fit quite snugly on her, but now slid a little around her legs and knees. She began reciting in her mind a partial hymn she had learned as a child for whenever she felt afraid, "*Though I walk through the shadow of the valley of death, I shall fear no evil...*" The feeling of the fabric sliding over her skin was launching her not into space but to the past in her mind where on many occasions she would be awakened by the sensation of something moving up her legs, separating the sheet and her clothes from her body to gain access to her intimate areas. A hand. A grown person's hand. Rough-skinned fingers softly caressing her inner thighs. She would become paralyzed. She couldn't move. Even if she did, what would she do? What could she say?

"Be a good girl," the man's voice would tell her in a low, soft voice, as someone who is telling a secret.

She knew what that meant. Lay there and pretend to be asleep. Don't say a thing. This is just a dream. The hand pushed harder up her thigh, slipping by under her thin night gown. She had learned to close her eyes and escape in her mind. It was the only way for her to do so. Any other way was impossible. Where could she run to in the village? Who would take her side against her father? No one would. No one could. Not even her mother. Or perhaps she could, but she chose not to, since few people opposed her father and lived to tell of it. If other grownups couldn't stand up to him, there was nothing an eleven-year-old girl could do to stop her tormentor. She worried that his groping might eventually turn into something else that she still had not been exposed to. Karina knew nothing about sex, but some intuitive sense told her that touching was just the beginning of what a man looked for when he explored the female body. She didn't know much about that, but one thing was clear: she had to run away. As insane and unspeakable as that seemed, she knew it was the only way.

> *"He makes me lie down in green pastures, he leads me beside quiet waters...I shall fear no evil."*

When she finally did run away, it was during the early morning on a school day. She boarded a stranger's truck. She had flagged it down asking for a ride to the next town to get medicine for her supposedly ailing mother, who had no one else who could care for her. When she arrived in the big town, she bought a ticket with the money she had stolen from her father's savings jar. He kept it in that sacred space carved out of the wall in the living room and covered up by a picture of his late mother, whom he adored as a saint and for whom he had built an altar at that same spot.

Karina boarded the train and headed out toward the city. She had heard rumors of organizations which helped migrating unaccompanied minors cross the border into the United States. Once in the U.S. she had been lucky enough to find a sponsor family who would eventually take her in when they met her at an immigrant shelter in McAllen, Texas. They had been volunteering with the refugee crisis relief effort there. They were an older couple, Linda and Jeremy from Sandusky, Ohio. They had been in the Rio Grande Valley in South Texas every winter for several years calling it home first as "Winter Texans," then full-timers after they had both retired from their teaching careers in Ohio public schools.

By any account, Karina's luck was uncommon. She was eventually able to gain residency and then naturalization as a United States citizen. Years later, before boarding the spaceship Pioneer, she had been asked by a reporter how she felt about leaving Earth. She responded:

"I look forward to starting a new life on Mars. I think it is a once-in-a-lifetime opportunity that no one should pass up. Certainly, I wouldn't dream of passing it up."

"But aren't you in the least worried about the fact that you will never be seeing your loved ones again? What about your family down in El Salvador?"

"I feel that I have lived enough of a life on Earth to a point where I can leave and not feel like I am lacking anything, or that I have left something undone. To me it is the exact same way that it felt like when I left my home country of El Salvador. I decided that it was time for me to go. I said my goodbyes in my own way to my family, and then I left and never looked back."

"What about your host family in the U.S.? Don't you feel like you will miss them, or feel sad by the prospect of never seeing them again, as well?" the reporter probed.

Karina seemed almost indifferent, unaffected emotionally, but she tried hard not to come across as cold and ungrateful. So, she would smile and nod, as if validating the importance of the reporter's questions, even though she privately did not feel that it was in any way relevant.

"I think what we are going to do on Mars is so much more important than how it will affect me, one person, because it will have an untold-of effect on the rest of humanity now and for many years to come. So, no I don't feel any fear or regrets about my decision."

The rumbling in the cockpit began to subside, and with it, Karina's thoughts, as well, began to fade into the background as she heard voices breaking through within her helmet. It was the voice of their mission commanders on the ground advising the crew that they could now unbuckle themselves and enjoy the feeling of weightlessness as it would be a few days until their ship docked with the auxiliary space tugboat called the Sling Blade. This ship would serve as a counter weight that would enable both vessels to spin in space tethered to each other, therefore creating gravitational forces that would allow the crew to have normal Earth-like conditions to walk freely about the ship.

"This is fun, isn't it," said Bianca, the forty-year-old woman (the only other woman of the four-member group).

"Yeah," Karina answered feigning coyness to disguise her disinterest. She felt that the purpose of disconnecting with Earth was to leave behind Earth-like behaviors. Engaging in small talk was very much something she wished to leave behind. She had her sights solely fixed on Mars. Karina couldn't even allow herself to enjoy the uniqueness of a journey aboard that ship; an experience which only a handful of humans had ever had before. She wasn't moved by the floating sensation, nor the small talk, nor by Leo's shenanigans as he suddenly came crashing-through between Karina and Bianca in a fetal position, shouting,

"Cannonball!"

Karina and Bianca looked at each other dismayed, eyes peeled, and then burst out laughing. Only then was Karina able to loosen up and be in the moment, although in the back of her mind she couldn't help but wonder how some people just seem to make themselves at home around others without having been expressly invited or welcomed. Leo had just assumed they would be willing to play. And without asking if they wished to join-in, he lunged himself at them, floating across the ship past them. She pondered the meaning behind it. At home on Earth she had learned that people who never asked but simply took usually ended up taking more than they deserved.

Emilio, on the other hand, seemed to be a lot more self-restrained. He stayed on the sidelines. Smiling softly as if to avoid being misinterpreted as making fun of people. Simply smiling. Nodding. Trying not to get in the way of the fun. Karina approached him and waved her hand to join them. Emilio simply nodded and smiled some more, unsure what to do or if to say something. So, he did nothing and stayed put. Karina thought that maybe his shyness was also tied to his past, like hers. She wondered what each of her crew members' stories were. Not that she truly wanted to get to know them in-depth. But simply to ponder, observe, and then deduce their stories. She felt she was much better at deciphering through the collection of clues than understanding through communication.

Karina had been lost again in thought when she was suddenly brought back to the present moment by Bianca saying,

"He's kind of cute, isn't he?"

Karina looked around as if they were in a room full of bachelors to scope out.

"Who?"

"Leo, of course. No offense, but that poor kid over there didn't even have a prayer on Earth much less on Mars. Am I right?" said Bianca with a giggle.

"Well I'm not interested in either of them."

"Oh, so you're not human," said Bianca with a wink.

"No, I mean, I pretty much resigned the rest of my life to celibacy. I don't really need a man to please me sexually or emotionally."

"Sure, I can understand that. But it is way more fun

when you have a man giving you a hand, if you know what I mean." Bianca giggled harder trying to see if Karina would join her. But Karina was not impressed. In fact, she felt somewhat sickened by the thought of Bianca actively enthralled in a sexual rendezvous. She didn't even fantasize about herself in that manner, much less would she enjoy partaking of the fantasies of another.

"Relax, kid. I'm just playing with you," Bianca finally said in a serious tone. "Is everything alright?"

Karina looked away into the distance and allowed a simple reply:

"Yeah."

"Look, I may talk all kinds of nonsense but the reality is I, too, am quite reserved. I pretty much gave up on love a long time ago. Actually, I gave up on men. It just seems like there is no pleasing them. You're either a whore for being sexually liberated, or a bore because you don't know how to do it. Either way they are going to cheat on you, leave you, beat you. It's a huge mess. Hey, maybe we're onto something going out there to Mars, huh? Start the first planet of celibate creatures that procreate only through artificial means. Eventually, we'll evolve to look like those little grey aliens with no sex organs or luscious lips. Just plain and simple-looking, asexual things."

Bianca looked at Karina warmly like a big sister offering advice to her younger sibling and trying to cheer her up. Karina smiled and nodded. Her head full of thoughts of being on Mars. How would she manage to get

82

alone time with such talkative, disruptive companions that pulled her out of her inner world where she spent most of her time?

After months of spaceflight, the ship approached the red planet, and the sleep capsules they had entered a month after docking with the Sling Blade began to reverse the cryogenic process allowing the crew to awaken from their long, deep slumber. They established their base camp and went to work on building their greenhouse and other facilities. Of course, this took little effort on their part in view of the fact that Mars Four Corporation had ensured that setup was almost entirely computer-guided and automated. Nothing was going to be left entirely to the crew. Too much was riding on the venture. But after months of solitude and rote exercises, the crew began to develop cabin fever. They became irritable. Snarking at each other.

One day, Bianca became severely ill. It was a mystery. No one knew what was happening to her. She was growing weaker by the hour until one day she was gone. Just like that. The first human to die on Mars. They mourned her loss more for themselves than for Bianca. Her death highlighted their vulnerability and desperate aloneness. Even Karina was feeling uncharacteristically homesick. She wondered if she could take back her words of not needing to be back on Earth for the rest of her life. Maybe she had gotten a bit ahead of herself. Maybe she could use the company of others. Perhaps even the company of a man.

They took Bianca's corpse out to start the first

Martian cemetery. Afterwards, the crew retreated to their camp trying to find the strength within themselves to face the harsh reality, which was suddenly dawning on them, that this was precisely what they had all signed up for to begin with: to come to Mars with no other purpose but to establish the first human colony and eventually die alone. Sure, there was always the reassuring idea in the back of their minds that Mars Four Corporation had intended them to be only the first of several pioneer crews to be sent to Mars. But that would not take place for maybe another decade or so.

The dwindling crew of three began to develop bonds that had been blocked by invisible walls set up primarily by Karina, who had been the one mostly bent on going it alone, seeking self-reliance, shunning intimacy. Now, she was open and welcoming. This was noticed easily by the men, especially Leo, who like a lion suddenly sensed something different in the air. The ice had thawed and the vibes had warmed as Karina called them to her with her eyes. Instantly, an evolutionary trait must have kicked-in and the two young men saw themselves at opposite ends of a love triangle with Karina at the top. They became excessively competitive for her attention.

For her part, Karina felt the need to be cherished, loved, and protected. Her natural inclination and attraction was toward Leo, who was what some would call an "alpha" type. Strong, tall, fit, and highly confident. Emilio, on the other hand, was the exact opposite of Leo in every way. He was skinny, average height, and way too shy. The choice was not difficult for Karina. But Emilio resented the vote of no confidence. He could tell that they had begun to have private relations. Perhaps in the middle of the night, as he slept. Maybe even when it was his turn to tend to the crops in the green house, which was not a two to three-minute job. It usually took them at least an entire hour to water the plants, and test the atmosphere in the large room for signs of radiation excess, which could ruin the crops. He couldn't pinpoint when, but he was sure they were sexually active.

Perhaps because of that realization, Emilio was showing an increasing willingness to challenge his much stronger, taller, tougher competitor, Leo. It was obvious in the way he was now questioning and sometimes even ridiculing Leo's input on the smallest things. Leo, at first, had not noticed the change in Emilio's attitude. But eventually, even he became aware of his condescension, and started pushing back firmly by imposing his will on matters instead of making suggestions as to how to proceed. Needless to say, what usually started with Emilio challenging a position typically ended by Leo getting in his face and forcing Emilio to back down and essentially obey his commands.

Karina took notice of the men's increasing animosity toward each other. She did not like it. She felt that she had tried as best she could to hide the fact that she was sexually intimate with Leo. But it was apparent that, somehow, Emilio knew of it and felt shunned. She became especially cognizant of the imbalance of the crew by how Emilio's treatment of her had also changed dramatically. At first, he had always been so sweet and delicate with her. But recently he had become much more volatile and snarky. Karina imagined that maybe it was due to an internal animal need for transcendence, which seems to drive the imperative to procreate, that the men became antagonistic toward each other in competition over her affection. She could not be certain. But what convinced her that something had to be done to correct the sudden drastic changes was that their hostilities had begun to spill over onto her. She was not comfortable with the idea of being at the center of a love triangle which had at the core of their problems the fact that she, Karina, the girl who ran away from her family because of sexual abuse, was having sexual relations with a man. There was just no way for them to reconcile their issues without doing what had to be done. Karina knew what that was. She concluded that it had to be her who would put a stop to it, especially since this situation only led to her feeling like she had become a simple sex object again, like when she was a child. She resolved to—just like when she was younger—take action for her own well-being.

Karina also realized that sex had changed everything for the worse. She knew the team needed to have harmony among them. After all, they were the only ones on Mars, and therefore, totally dependent on one another. They had to be able to coexist without constantly being in an adversarial position. The men had no say in the matter. They would have to accept her decision. She sat them both down and explained,

"I have made a terrible mistake. As you are quite aware," she said, turning to Emilio, "Leo and I have been getting...closer to each other than would be convenient for our group dynamic. I think it may have been due to the loss of Bianca. It made me feel so alone and depressed. Vulnerable. I felt like I needed to have a stronger bond with someone who could offer me not just friendship, but also a sense of protection. But I realize that that is a fallacy. We are all going to die one day no matter who is with you or where you are. I am ready to confront my fears by myself."

She turned to Leo at this point and noticed his look of incredulity. He may have thought that she was making a gesture to throw off Emilio, who had been the most affected in a negative way by their courtship. So, Karina made it a point to look straight in Leo's eyes so there would be no mistaking her words and her true intent. She said, gazing into his soul,

"Please forgive me for having allowed things to come this far. If it had not been for my moment of weakness, none of this infighting between you two would be taking place. We need to be a strong team. A team whose members take care of one-another. Who look out for each other. And you and I having this type of relationship is not conducive to that goal. After all, it is our priority to make the mission of colonizing this planet a success. For us and for all other crews to come. You and I cannot continue down the path of intimacy. It would jeopardize the mission. I hope you will understand."

Emilio seemed resigned to that fate, while Leo appeared unconvinced by her argument. He was not the type of guy who was accustomed to rejection. Karina knew this intuitively. But, regardless of his apparent displeasure, he said nothing and acquiesced with a silent bow of his head.

The days seemed to slow down to a snail's pace.

87

The sun hanging on the sky longer. Sunsets redder and stubborn. They had stopped counting hours and days a long time ago. After Bianca passed away, they had attempted to revive the broken communications system which had been damaged on the landing. No luck. They had to make do on their own guidance and self-reliance. Karina thought that perhaps that had been the reason why she had begun to change her approach toward sex and men. After Bianca's death, there was no one to rely on but the only two other people with her on that far away planet, Leo and Emilio. That and the fact that being trapped in such a small enclosure for what felt like an eternity drove her to madness. It was a small space they inhabited. The entire facility measured only about the size of a two-bedroom apartment. It only appeared larger because there were also the greenhouse and other compartments. But those rooms were so crowded that they provided no comfort as living or working areas.

One day, Leo recruited Emilio to assist him on an expedition to a remote location which they had been surveying with the assistance of a drone equipped with a camera. Karina heard the discussion and began suiting up believing that she, too, would be needed on the journey.

"You stay here, Karina," said Leo authoritatively.

Karina looked at him puzzled and asked, "Why?"

"We'll need someone to operate the drone by remote while we are out on foot. You'll be our eyes in the sky," Leo replied conclusively.

"I can do that from the rover, as well. What would be the difference?"

"Exactly. What's the difference?" quipped Leo, giving her a wink and a nod as if the matter had been settled.

For Karina, the matter had absolutely not been settled. She felt the need to fire back and insist on going. As a matter of fact, she felt like simply suiting up and loading herself into the rover. There would be nothing he could do about it if she had decided to take it that far. Nothing, that is, except maybe literally ripping her butt out of that vehicle and just throwing her back into the base camp. After all, he really was that strong. But she decided not to go to those lengths.

Instead, she concluded that perhaps this was a "man" thing. A way for two males going out on a trip to form bonds, or do whatever men do when they are alone with each other. She had seen this back when she was a child in El Salvador and her father would always shout at her to go back inside the house with "the women" when he was hanging out with his buddies in the back yard burning wood, cooking meat, and drinking cheap Brandy.

So, Karina resigned herself to accepting the task of drone handler from base. She waited at the control room for the call from the men out on the Martian terrain. It had been quite a while since she had been out on an expedition. Every time she had gone out, she found the quiet solitude of the barren planet thoroughly enjoyable. No traffic. No terrible fumes congesting the nostrils and dizzying the

89

head. No strays or loose dogs growling and threatening to bite her. No men insinuating themselves to her with disgusting catcalls. That was the absolute worst thing in the world for her...well, that and being touched without her consent, of course. She realized she liked going out there so much that she made a determination. She would tell her fellow crew members that, no matter what, on the next expedition out to the far reaches of their colony, she would be coming along and she would take no objections, or rejections, or advice against that idea. The decision was made. They would just have to live with it.

Karina had been busy thinking about the Martian landscape and envisioning herself talking to her companions (especially Leo, who took it upon himself to declare himself their leader) about her decision. She had practiced the words, the tone of her voice, and even her physical positioning. Everything would count. The guys seeing her as a junior crew member—a weaker link—was her own doing, she thought. Letting herself be influenced by the fear of isolation and of dying alone on Mars had only served to allow the men to treat her like the proverbial damsel in distress. But not anymore. No more Ms. Nice Girl. She had always been, and would continue to be, her own knight in shining armor.

She was still caught up in these thoughts when she realized that hours had passed and still no call-in from the rover for the air cover. Without their coordinates, she could not fly the thing out to meet them and see what they were up to. She attempted to radio them but it appeared that their receivers were off. Then she thought of using the Mars GPS to locate them. But somehow the rover's beacon did not register on the device. Something must have gone wrong, she thought. She kept trying the various instruments to no avail. Then she decided that she would use the drone after all, since it couldn't hurt and could lead her to find the rest of her crew.

For an entire hour, she flew that drone all over the sector which Leo had stated they would be exploring. Not a sign of the rover nor of the men was evident. Nervousness was beginning to set in. Her worst fear since the loss of Bianca to a mysterious cause was seemingly coming true. She would end up completely alone on the red planet for who knows how long. It could be years, or even decades until another crew arrived. What if war broke out among the super powers? What would happen then to the Mars Four Corporation's plans to send additional crews of colonists to join her? It would be very likely that all space exploration would cease. This is what was streaming through her mind's eye so vividly that she felt like running outside shouting at the top of her lungs looking for her comrades. The feeling of panic was so overwhelming that she felt like she would lose her sanity at any moment when suddenly there was a blip on the GPS device. Hope had returned. After nearly an entire day having her crew members missing out on the Martian landscape, she was so relieved and joyous at the prospect of being able to contact them again and have a word.

She radioed the rover and Leo was the one to respond.

"Where the hell have you two been? I had been worried out of my goddamned mind!"

"Sorry about that," said Leo sounding sincerely apologetic. "It must have been that our systems were disrupted after we drove the rover into this huge underground cave."

"Do you know the absolute terror you guys have put me through? Oh my God! I thought I was going to end up by myself and die alone on this God-forsaken planet."

"Karina. I got some bad news." Leo said after a brief silence.

"What's wrong?"

"I'm coming back to base...alone."

"What do you mean alone? Where is Emilio?"

"There was an accident. When we reached a certain point in the cave we realized we had come to a cliff. If it hadn't have been for Emilio's quick reaction, I would have driven us both off the cliff and into the abyss. Who knows how far down it went."

"So, what happened to him? You said he saw the danger ahead. What happened?!" Karina's voice was sounding increasingly distressed at the prospect of having lost yet another of there already shrinking crew of colonists.

"Well, we both decided to get off and try to look for a path which we might take on foot either down into the canyon or around it and further into the cave. When Emilio opened his door, he headed off in one direction and I went the opposite way. I ordered him to come back and follow me, but you know how he's been lately. I don't think he had gotten over us having been together. In any case, at some point I turned around to call out to him again, since I had lost sight of him completely, but before I could say his name I heard him scream. I quickly headed back around as fast as I could. I searched for him but could not find him. The only thing I found was his access card to the pods right at the edge of the cliff. He must have gotten too close and fell in. I called out to him in case he had survived the fall but had no response. There was nothing else I could do but head back to base."

By this point, Karina was speechless. Leo called out for her over the radio, but she could only manage a hum to signal that she was still there. He told her that he would just wait until he got back to base so they could talk more about it. She responded absentmindedly with a simple "Uh-huh."

Days passed and Karina could still not reconcile what had taken place. It seemed so surreal. So arbitrary. Was the universe upset at them for attempting to revive a planet that it had long declared dead? Was God being vengeful toward them for defying the natural limitations He had set on the human species? After all, He had never intended for humans to exist on planets other than Earth. If that had been the case, then God would have made several Earths. Not just the one we know.

Many thoughts passed through her increasingly tormented mind. In spite of the fact that Leo had explained how Emilio had tragically met his end, she could not help but to think that it was all due to her mistake of inadvertently pitting them against each other. She wondered—even though deep down she thought it an absurd proposition—whether the two men would have done a better job of looking out for one-another if there had never been any form of animosity or competition between them for her attention. Of course, it was a ridiculous thought. But it was still one that plagued her. Even though she had always seen herself as someone who would be happiest in the absence of all people around her (which was what had led her to join the Mars Four Corporation to begin with) she discovered that deep down she was a very warm and caring person, who wanted nothing but good things to come to others, even if she didn't really want anything to do with them.

During the early evening of the third night since Emilio's accident, as they were relaxing next to a window overlooking the sunset, a figure jumped up at them against the window. They were startled to see that it was none other than their lost companion. Instinctively, Karina quickly maneuvered to let him in. Once inside, Leo was at a loss for words. Emilio pointed at him as if to say something but seemingly couldn't catch his breath. Karina tried to decipher his unintelligible mouthing. She then opted to go get their health kit in the hopes of administering some first aid. When Karina was making her way back she could hear a commotion inside the room where she had left the two men but couldn't open the door. After a very brief struggle she managed to slide it open and saw the scene before her: Leo on top of Emilio choking him. She said, shouting at the top of her lungs,

"Stop it!"

"He attacked me!" said Leo briefly letting go. Emilio tried to regain his composure, but was still too weak and coughing excessively to be able to speak.

Karina looked at both of them not knowing what to think. But something told her things weren't as simple as they seemed. Perhaps it was the fact that up to that point everything she had known about Emilio's accident and this incident had come from only one source: Leo. She looked over at Emilio who was about to speak, reaching a hand out to her, but Leo used this as a pretext to attack Emilio once again, making it seem as if he were thwarting an attack against Karina.

Of course, Karina had not seen it that way, so she rose to her feet from where she had been kneeling alongside them, and commanded Leo to release him. Leo ignored her. Karina ran over to the inventory closet in the hallway grabbed the 20 lbs. fire extinguisher and swung it hard against the back of Leo's head. The thump was so loud that she immediately jumped back as she saw his body go limp and flop to the side, slamming on the floor like a heavy bag of cement.

"He's dead," said Emilio looking at Leo and rubbing his own neck, still choking on a cough.

"That can't be. I didn't mean to kill him. I didn't know what to do. He wanted to kill you."

"You did the right thing, Karina."

"But he did say you attacked him. Why did you attack him?"

"No. I did not. It was all a lie. Did he tell you what happened out there? Why I didn't come back?"

"He told me you had an accident and fell off a cliff. There was nothing he could do to save you or retrieve your body."

"Horrible lies."

"What do you mean? What really happened."

"Well, let's just say that this was not the first time he had attempted to kill me."

Karina looked at him intently, and although she said nothing, her eyes made it clear that she had doubted all along Leo's version of events. She had intuited that something was way off about how he had so conveniently ended up the one to come back unscathed from that excursion. It was clear to her that both men wanted her. But what was also clear was that only one of them looked capable of doing anything and everything to keep her to himself; that was Leo.

They took Leo's body out and buried him in the slowly-growing Martian colony cemetery. There was no ceremony. No eulogy. Life was losing all meaning on that planet. The death of Leo had further pushed the sanity of the slowly disappearing crew to the brink. It was Karina who was taking most of the psychological hit. First, the loss of her friend and quasi-older sister, Bianca. Then, the apparent accidental death of Emilio, which turned out to be an attempted murder and a ruse. Finally, her sudden act of violence against an imminent threat that lead to Leo's death. No matter how much Emilio tried to console her by rationally explaining how she really had had no other choice, she felt a terrible weight on her shoulders. The guilt was tearing her apart.

"Who knows what he had in mind for you after killing me again, right?" Emilio asked Karina in an attempt to reassure her that, indeed, her actions had been warranted.

Still, there was just no way she could just put Leo's death out of her mind. This whole Mars experience had turned out to be a lot more trouble than even life on Earth had been for a young Central American girl. But the one promising thing about Mars was that it had one very sweet guy that any girl could trust and feel safe around. Emilio was ever more attentive with Karina. He listened to her. He reassured her. He let her lean on him in every way without making her fear the prospect of him turning around and expecting or demanding something in return for his kindness.

Emilio, for his part, began to feel like Karina did not even notice him as a man. Quite like before, when Leo was around. The truth was that he was not at all as affected by the loss of the group's alpha male. In fact, he felt relief at not having to worry about being second to anyone. But that still did not seem to convince Karina that she could

97

lean on him not only for emotional support, but for much, much more. How could he trigger in her the desire to want to be with a man again...with him? Was he not manly enough to evoke that inner goddess in her?

He pondered the question in the nights while lying in bed next to her and feeling his body pleading with him to grab her and bring her closer, close enough to press upon. But he was no predator, he thought to himself. How could he just take her when she appeared so far removed from any desire for sexual intimacy? In fact, Karina would lie next to him recounting stories of her childhood. Her family. The village she grew up in. The first day she arrived on American soil; how wonderful and promising it had all felt. He liked to listen to her. She was a sweet girl, after all. All she would talk about were her experiences being a kid. Occasionally, she would insert topics about puberty revolving around her changes and how boys took notice. Then she would venture into stories of boyfriends. These he did not mind, although they did bring up the question in his mind: had they ever been "boyfriend and girlfriend," how would she talk about him if she were in conversation with someone else about her experiences with lovers?

Then Emilio would come back from his musings after she had fallen asleep next to him and slowly run his eyes along the traces of her figure. The curve of her hips. The shape of her breasts as they pushed against the jumpsuit. Only after he had confirmed that she was fully asleep would he slide down his hand toward his groin area. Emilio pressed upon himself as he reached toward her head to smell her hair. The desire became so compelling that on one occasion he reached out to touch her as he simultaneously touched himself. He must have gotten so excited that he lost self-control momentarily and squeezed hard enough so that Karina awoke to the feeling of being eleven years old again, being groped and violated in her sleep.

"What are you doing?"

"Oh, I'm sorry."

"Look Emilio, I don't want you to take this the wrong way, but I just feel that I could never go back to being intimate with anyone. Not after all that has happened. I hope you can understand."

"What would be so wrong with us being intimate? I don't get it. You used to be intimate before, remember? With Leo. Well now he's gone, and I'm here. Besides, it's not like we don't care for each other. We share everything about ourselves. I feel like I know you so well. We are almost like a married couple."

"I just don't feel that it would be appropriate for us to do anything like that. It just makes me feel so guilty. Leo is dead. I think he tried to kill you just to keep me to himself. And for us to even talk about having sex now when all of these things have happened because of how messed up things got between us, I don't know. It just doesn't feel right, you know?"

"Karina, I love you."

"No, no, no. Emilio, you do not love me. I am just a

messed-up girl. I could never have those feelings for you. You are a lot more like my best friend or even a brother."

"A brother!? How can you claim to feel like I'm your brother? I can't believe you said that!"

"I'm sorry, Emilio. I did not mean to offend you. I really care about you. I think that you are a very sweet guy. You deserve someone who can love you like you want a woman to love you. I cannot love you like that. Besides, if you are basing this on what happened between me and Leo, my feelings have not changed. I told you both I still believe that was a mistake. I really don't want to ruin our friendship, Emilio."

"Wow. That is just brilliant. You can't love me like I want a woman to love me. I 'deserve' someone that can give me that, huh? I'm sorry, do you see a horde of women lined up to give me the kind of love that I want? Let me know where I can find them on this barren wasteland. I'm sure they will be eager to please me."

"Emilio, let's not do this. We are all we have for the meantime. Eventually there will be others. We both know that they will be sending more people. And when they do, it's very likely there will be someone among them with whom you will fall in love. Trust me. We should get some rest and talk about it in the morning."

"I'll tell you what we are going to do. We are going to role-play. You can't love me like I want you to, right? Apparently, you didn't love Leo like he wanted you to, either. Did you? Because, as far as I recall, you put out that

100

flame like nothing. That could only mean that you were acting as someone you are not. Therefore, you are a great actress. So, here's what you are going to do: you are going to act as if you really want me, and I am going to do whatever I want with you because I am a man!"

"Emilio stop it!"

"Scared, huh? Good. That's good. Go with that feeling. Now do as I say. Remove your suit."

"Emilio, no!"

Karina moved away fast, as she struggled to her feet still drowsy from her interrupted sleep. Emilio was quicker to rise up, closing the gap between them and grabbing her by a wrist, but she managed to shake him off.

"I am a man. You are a woman. You will please me because as a man, I deserve to be pleased!"

"Don't do this, Emilio. Not you. Not you, too. Please…please, Emilio," she implored, feeling foolish for having once thought that she was saved from sexual predation the day she escaped the backward ways of her original homeland where her father had abused her.

"Look at me. You are mine," Emilio said, grabbing Karina by the shoulders and squeezing so hard, she literally felt the bruises forming on her skin. She tried to fight him off, but he pulled out a screwdriver from his pocket and made sure she had a clear view of it, as he grabbed her long, brown hair and used it to pull her close to him. The

101

warning was not lost on her when she had the screwdriver inches from her face.

Wild-eyed and completely ignoring her appeals for self-restraint, he continued, "We were meant to be. You and me. We are this new world's Adam and Eve. We are going to populate this new world and make it in our own image," he concluded with a fire in his eyes that Karina had never seen before. It was the devil inside him advising the once sweet and gentle man she had come to know and trust.

That night Karina died. Not in body, but in spirit. To her, the proof was undeniable that there was just no escaping the evil that lurks in the hearts of men. She had tried. She had traveled nearly forty million miles in an attempt to escape it. But she found out that it had accompanied her in disguise as a friend. There was no hope for mankind. She knew this unequivocally. This Martian odyssey had led her on a journey straight back in time and space landing her in El Salvador again as an eleven-year-old being asked to lie there and be a "good girl". Likewise, for the rest of that tragic night on Mars she turned her spirit to God as she closed her eyes and traveled in here mind, leaving her body on the physical plane to be handled by unwelcomed hands.

"...thy rod and thy staff they comfort me."

The following morning, the sun rays splashed red fire on the horizon casting a glow on Karina's face which was fixated on the window looking out into the Martian desert. If there had been anyone else around to witness her face from the outside, they could have thought her to be a

102

statue sitting there with a solemn, hopeless look of despair. Emilio lay asleep in the private quarters oblivious to the turmoil that his captive was experiencing.

Karina got up from the floor with an unexpected zeal in her step and a determination in her mind. She walked toward the interior of the pod looking for the command and control room. It came-in handy not only since she needed to get away from Emilio, but because the solution to her problem was within that very room. Karina searched the control board for a particular panel of buttons. She was dialing those buttons when she was surprised to hear Emilio's soft, effeminate voice.

"Karina, where are you? I've got something to tell you."

"There is nothing to talk about."

"Look, first of all I want to apologize for my behavior. I don't know what took over me last night. Please forgive me. Karina...I am asking you for forgiveness."

"There is nothing to forgive."

"Karina, please don't cut me off like that. We have to talk about what happened last night. We are going to live together for as long as we can manage. It is important that we get these things sorted out. We need each other to survive."

"I wouldn't worry about that. There is no need to sort anything out when our time here will come to an end sooner rather than later."

"What are you talking about? Karina, what did you do? Open up! Karina, open up right now!"

"Don't you see? There is no way for us to live together. You have no control over yourself. Even in these, our final moments, you are raising your voice. What's next? Are you going to threaten to beat me again? I have deactivated the oxygen production system. I have remotely expelled the rest of the fuel in the tanks. This facility will cease to operate soon, and within just a few moments after that, we will die of asphyxiation. All is as it should be for a failed mission such as ours."

"No, Karina. You cannot do this! You cannot make that decision by yourself. What about me? I don't want to die. I deserve to live!" The urgency and disbelief in Emilio's voice said it all. He must have been squirming outside that door. Terrified of dying. Resembling in no way the tough guy she had confronted the previous night.

"I deserved to live, too, Emilio. To live a happy life. And you killed me last night. Now there is nothing else to do here but die."

As if on cue, at the moment she uttered those dire words, the humming and vibrations coming through the walls of the complex came to a halt and the lights turned off. Being that it was still early morning, the faint sunlight managed to illuminate just enough of the interior so that one could still make sense of where things were, since the facility was equipped with windows on the ceiling to make

104

use of the Martian sunlight and conserve energy for night-time usage, or for stormy days.

Emilio began to ram his upper body against the door to the control room. It proved difficult to break down not only because he was not a very strong man, but primarily owing to the fact that the door was not on hinges for it to swing open. It was on a rail for it to slide open and shut. He went just a few steps ahead to the inventory closet in the hallway—the same one Karina had visited when she picked up the fire extinguisher to bash Leo over the head—and grabbed a hammer. He threw all his weight behind it and in just three blows, he managed to break a small opening through the door, just enough to slide his hand through and press the button that released the locking mechanism. Karina jumped off the chair ready to fight to the death. He lunged forward into the room and with an agile maneuver threw Karina on the ground landing on top of her. Emilio grabbed her by the shoulders and shook her saying

"What did you do? What did you do!?"

"I did what had to be done. What is the use of this colony if the same injustices and fears that we thought we left behind have followed us here? It's useless! I don't want to live like that."

"You bitch! You killed us. You killed us!"

He moved his hands from Karina's shoulders up toward her neck and began to squeeze. Emilio could hear her gasping for air as she tried to fend him off unsuccessfully. The growing flood of light had managed to brighten the room just enough so that Emilio could make out Karina's perfect features clearly now. She was still the most beautiful woman he had ever been with, aside from being the only woman he'd been with. Karina went limp. Not due to having stopped living, but because she was ready to die.

Quite unexpectedly, she felt the tightness around her neck loosen up. She coughed and coughed struggling to grab some air to breath and make sense of what was going on. She wondered why Emilio had stopped himself from killing her?

Emilio started chuckling at first to himself, but then louder until he filled the room with his laughter bouncing off the walls. Karina concluded that he had simply gone mad. She waited for the right moment and when he seemed distracted Karina quickly jumped up, grabbed the hammer that he had placed on the control panel and with the blunt part of it struck Emilio across the temple laying him out like a boxer being knocked out cold. Yet Emilio hadn't been knocked unconscious. He tried to sit up but barely got to his elbow on which he leaned, grabbing his temple with his other hand as blood started gushing out, running down the length of his forearm. He looked at Karina and said,

"It's so ironic. The lengths I went to just to have you to myself. And now that I have succeeded in doing that, you casually pull the plug and kill us." He kept chuckling, wholly amused by his musings.

"What do you mean the lengths that you went to?"

106

"You really do like to play the innocent victim, don't you. Fine. I'll humor you. Here," he said, handing Karina a vile he pulled out from his pocket.

"What's this?" She asked, though in the back of her mind she suspected what it could be.

"Exactly what it looks like. A little vile of poison. What do you think made Bianca so sick? I would have used it on Leo as well, but you took good care of that one. A much better method of disposal, I might add. I hated that guy. He thought he was such a stud. Big tough guy. Jerks like him were the reason I left Earth. And to come and end up on Mars in the presence of the thing I could not stand on the home planet, well I was not going to put up with that."

"Why would you do that? You monster! Why are you telling me this now?"

"Isn't it obvious?" he said momentarily taking his blood-soaked hand and showing it to Karina, as if she had not noticed his wound. "It's my last confession before I meet my maker. And I also wanted to tell you simply to see the look on your face. I got to tell you, it's gold. I wouldn't trade this moment for the world." Emilio leaned back to breath hard as he felt another laughing spell overcoming him.

Karina stood there watching this cold-blooded killer laughing after having confessed to have killed Bianca. She remembered how sweet Bianca had been toward her, acting like her big sister by being kind and understanding of her.

107

Even though she had been completely selfish the entire time Bianca had been around. Her eyes could not hold back the tears any longer and she broke down with the image of Bianca's corpse on her mind.

"Oh, come on. Don't cry, Karina. You're going to ruin the moment."

"Don't speak. I don't want to know anything else. I don't want to hear you anymore. I'm getting out of here," she said, as she exited the room to retrieve her suit. She came back to the entrance simply to keep an eye on Emilio and make sure he didn't attempt to escape, as well. She had decided that she would suit up and take the rover to their auxiliary ship stationed far from their landing site. There was no way she could blast off and catch the Sling Blade in space. She simply did not have the technical skills to conduct the entire procedure on her own. But at least she would use it as her base for as long as she could hold out in the hopes that maybe one of the other crews arrived. It was a long shot, but it was her only chance.

"And where do you think you're going, young lady? There's still more to reveal. Don't you want to know what truly happened the day Leo and I went on our little expedition?"

"I said don't speak. I don't want to know what happened. I don't care. Because of you Leo is dead. Just shut up!" She yelled in exasperation.

"Because of me? Beg your pardon? Well, isn't that convenient of you to crack a man's skull in two and then blame the other guy for it. Tsk, tsk, Karina."

"It was you. You made me think that he was the one trying to kill you." Karina realized she was mentally exhausted playing out in her head how things had happened which led her to side with Emilio instead of Leo.

"You poor girl. You are obviously torturing your pretty, little head trying to find the answers. Just sit back and let me fill you in on the details. Believe me you will feel better," Emilio invited her to sit tilting his head toward the chair at the control panel and pointing with his chin. She did not accept the offer and simply stood looking at the floor, looking at nothing, as she finished zipping up and securing her oxygen mask.

"Let's just say," continued Emilio as if retelling a great story, "...I was very clever at staging my disappearance (which actually wasn't that hard considering that Leo was a complete meathead—easily fooled). When he went out looking for me, calling out my name like a big dumb animal, I came back to the rover and hid in the suit compartments. He never thought to look for me in there. What an idiot. Anyway, the plan was to somehow sneak in to the base and slowly begin poisoning him as well. Operating in the shadows, like a ninja. Like a ghost. Only after seeing him close to death, I would miraculously return, having been saved by an act of God!" He laid himself back down and tried to follow up his statement with a laugh, but the loss of blood was starting to affect his strength, allowing him only a simple giggle.

"You would have totally eaten that up," Emilio

109

continued seemingly breathlessly, letting his arms fall to the sides. "I knew it wouldn't have worked if I simply killed him out there in the desert. You would have been suspicious, especially since you knew I couldn't stand the fact that you had given yourself to him," he looked at her in disgust as he said this and paused momentarily. He then continued with his confession,

"Anyway, I wasn't wrong at all. I mean, you proved it when you killed him thinking he was the aggressor. Isn't that something?" He said stopping again and giving her a wink before proceeding, "But the first night back, when I was sure you two were asleep, I tried to come in the building but realized that I had dropped my entry card out in the desert. There was no way to go back and find it. I had to think fast. I had to wait for the right moment. That's why the next evening, after observing you all day long, I jumped out of nowhere at the window where you were sitting. And the rest is history..." Emilio said, grinning wickedly.

"Enough!" said Karina, finally. Even if he had intended to continue with the mental torture, Emilio seemed to be losing consciousness. He shifted from wickedness to a full reversal back to when he was the quiet, shy, nice guy. He noticeably struggled for air now, as the pool of blood grew around his head.

"Karina..."Emilio called out weakly. "Water. Please..."

Karina felt a vague sense of compassion for a man who had proven that no person, no matter how good they seem, can ever be trusted. She realized that he was

110

agonizing from the wound she had caused. Karina felt obligated to grant him one last act of compassion. When she returned with the glass of water, she took the vile of poison and emptied its contents in it. She knelt beside Emilio and lifted his head to help him drink. He took only a few sips and she laid his head back down, then she rose back to her feet ready to leave. Before she could turn away, she took one more look at Emilio, who by now seemed to be choking on his own saliva. The dose had been so large that it multiplied the symptoms Bianca had experienced by one hundred times. The choking, gurgling sounds suddenly subsided, and Emilio exhaled profoundly for the last time in his life.

Karina turned away from him and closed her eyes. Horrified at Emilio's revelations and what they implied about her own part in all of it, Karina couldn't help but feel the entire weight of the tragedies on Mars choking the life out of her more than the lack of oxygen and the poison had snuffed the life out of Emilio. That made three people who had died in some way because of her. No matter how vile a person he was, she realized she did not have the right to have ended his life. She covered her face ashamed at herself. The tears flowing down pooling inside her tight-fitting oxygen mask.

"...and I shall dwell in the house of the lord forever."

She recited to herself the last part of the hymn she could remember as she took the cup with the remaining mixture of water and poison drinking until the last drop. She had been holding the mask up then placed it back on her face more out of habit than for any other reason. She looked up and saw the Martian sun appearing through the window in the ceiling, and said as if talking to it, "The point of it all was to discover the boundaries of the character of men. Can it be stretched? Can we escape its terrible flaws? The answer is no. Mission accomplished."

Karina violently yanked off the oxygen mask from her head, and flung it across the room as she began to feel a strange sense of drowsiness accompanied by a knot in her throat that made her grimace, closing her eyes tightly. When she opened them again, she was back in the cockpit of the spaceship Pioneer, which she had boarded not too long ago. She could feel the rumbling and vibrations of the jets exploding with a fury that burned the ground as if in retaliation for a past offense. When she saw herself lifting off the ground, Karina realized that it was her inner self leaving her body. Turning back one last time, she now saw herself lying on the floor next to Emilio. At that moment, her whole life started playing back and forth in her mind as if projected from an old-style movie reel being rewound and fast forwarded. She turned again to face the sky and flew her last trip across the cosmos, headed directly into the Martian sun.

Martian Harvest

The proud couple stood side by side watching as the ship their son and daughter had just boarded took flight into the red planet's sky carrying the surplus tribute of minerals and other products now produced on Mars after the first 50 years of successful colonization. In that ship were also a certain number of other Martian citizens going to Earth for the first time. Most of them were teenagers and only a few adults in their mid-thirties. They had been selected by the Earth-Mars commission to go to Earth for an extended stay in which they would have the chance to see the old world of their grandparents and also attend Earth schools and training academies. It wasn't that these things were unavailable on Mars, but the thought was that the program would allow for continued close ties between Earth and Mars communities, therefore maintaining a strong bond. The real incentive for Martians was that they were also promised a handsome grant which they could use to finance not only their stay on Earth but also the acquisition of goods of all kinds which they would be allowed to take back to their Martian homeland. All in all, it was a dream-come-true for any of the chosen ones. And indeed, most young people on Mars were eager to sign up for that lottery and hope to be lucky enough to be chosen.

The couple, Mary and Joe, standing by the large window that overlooked the launch pad kept their eyes on the ship as it reached for the heavens. They began to walk

113

away after the craft became little more than a speck in the distance. In their minds the thought of their son and daughter, 17 and 16 years old respectively, going to Earth and having wonderful adventures was a tremendous prospect which brought a slight smirk to their faces as they looked at each other. Sure, they would miss their kids but life on Mars had taught them to be tough about matters of the heart and the fleeting nature of existence. The commonly-held view among Martians, was that nothing lasts forever, and no one truly ever possessed anything in life...not even their own lives.

Mary and Joe were headed back to their posts awaiting them, for no one on Mars ever lacked for work. Although 50 years of colonization (and the great migration from Earth coupled with the baby boom of just 20 years prior) had produced a population explosion that was quite impressive and supplied an ample labor force for all the tasks of colonization, still the work never ceased. It seemed that the more hands became available, the more work was found for those new hands. Nonetheless, this seeming surplus of humanity on Mars did allow for the luxury of such a program as the Earth-Mars Exchange, since it did focus mostly on taking young Martians. So, although there was much work for everyone, Mary and Joe were happy to cover for any work due on behalf of their children.

As they entered their sector of the Mars settlement, a figure jumped at them from behind a door, startling the couple. They quickly identified the man, however. It was Benjamin. He wasn't a close friend by any stretch, but they knew enough about him to consider him an acquaintance.

"Mary. Joe. What have you done!?"

"Excuse me?" said Mary.

"You should not have let your children sign up for that trip to Earth!"

"Why not? It's a great opportunity," replied Joe.

"I've heard things. Bad things. About that program," Benjamin warned, careful not to raise his voice, and constantly scoping out his surrounding as if expecting to be apprehended at any moment.

Mary and Joe looked intently at Benjamin as he related a terrible tale of treachery on the part of the Earth-Mars Exchange program. They looked occasionally back at each other in a nervous apprehension, having only moments before seen their children blast off into an uncertain future. Sure, they had been promised their return. But nothing in life is ever guaranteed...nothing.

Benjamin continued with desperation in his eyes: "...and once they are supposedly on Earth, they never return. When was the last time you saw a ship coming back with the same crew as they took?"

Mary interjected before he could continue: "Just last month the U.S.S. Harvester arrived from Earth bringing back several young people who had been away for at least four years. And there have been other arrivals, though the program is relatively new. But I've seen it happen. We've seen it for ourselves," Mary said with conviction in her voice as she corrected herself to include her husband as a witness to her testimony.

"Yes. You are right to point that out," said Benjamin.

"But did you get a good look at exactly who came back? They were mainly the sons and daughters of our Martian representatives. But the common people's kids haven't had the same luck. According to officials, they are still on Earth. Yet no one is allowed to attempt to contact them and no one is allowed to even inquire about them. Believe me. I have tried. They refuse to tell me anything about my Sandra. They just tell me that she is fine and that I simply need to return to my post and wait until there's news from Earth. But it's a lie. They are hiding something."

"Oh Benjamin," said Mary speaking in a much softer, caring tone. "I had no idea you had a daughter. When did she leave?"

"Eight years ago."

"Eight years? Impossible!" exclaimed Joe incredulously. "She should have been back already, shouldn't she?"

"Of course," said Benjamin. "She should have been back four years ago. And yet, here we are eight years later and still I have heard nothing nor seen anything about her to confirm their claim that she is fine. And I just don't know what else to do. I need to know that she is okay.

There has to be some way."

"I'm sure there is some way you could find out about her, Benjamin," Mary spoke tenderly as she gently placed her hand on his shoulder in a show of empathy.

Benjamin looked up at Mary as he felt her touch, and spoke trying to contain the crystalline liquid filling his eyes from running down his face. He said,

"I hoped there would be someone who could help me. But there isn't. We are nobodies. We have no one to defend us. No one to stand up for our rights. Think of it. It's the perfect situation. They can literally do whatever they want with us or to us and no one is going to bat an eye. Not here and much less on Earth. We are worse off than even the animals. At least they have interest groups that try to protect their rights. But us? We are completely on our own. Powerless. Voiceless."

Joe was beginning to look impatient as he stood there listening to Benjamin paint such a bleak picture of their situation. As he saw it, it was possible that Benjamin's daughter, Sandra, could have found herself in the midst of several different destinies. She could have found love on Earth and started a family. Since the trip to Earth was sponsored, and she was obviously not of a wealthy family, she might have just realized that the only way to return home to Mars would be by parting forever with, potentially, the love of her life. And, likewise, if she wanted to be with her lover, she would have to say goodbye to her past life on Mars. Either way, she would have been

117

stuck between a rock and a hard place, as the saying goes. Therefore, regardless of the decision she made, the outcome would be one of pain by cutting ties with one person or another in her life permanently.

It was obvious to Joe that that explanation made most sense and that Benjamin's daughter simply had chosen to stay on Earth. But of course, he thought he shouldn't be so blunt with Benjamin, who was clearly in distress. Joe made his conclusions to himself and gathered strength from that, since now it was their son and daughter who had gone to Earth and possibly could find themselves at a similar crossroads which could compel them to choose to stay and never see Mary and Joe again. There was a strange comfort in his reasoning, although the prospect of their children choosing to never return was undeniably unsettling. This softened up Joe a little towards Benjamin and his plight.

"Look, Benjamin, I totally understand your concern and truly feel for you," he said as he took Mary by the hand as if signaling that they must get going. He put his free hand on Benjamin's shoulder and continued:

"We must have faith in the knowledge that our sons and daughters are individuals capable of making their own choices and decisions. Even if those decisions mean we will never see them again."

Mary turned to Joe with a look of dismay. She had not expected that from him.

"Joe! Please, honey. Have some sympathy. The man

118

is in pain."

"I am being sympathetic. Look, Benjamin. I don't mean to be rude. But isn't it possible that your daughter may have chosen to stay on Earth?"

Benjamin looked intently at Joe as if considering the possibility.

"Think about it. She was a young lady when she left, wasn't she?" asked Joe. Benjamin signaled yes with a nod and a look of odd curiosity.

"So, now she is a fully-grown woman. Capable of finding love. Or choosing to stay for any number of other reasons. The point is that we raise our children to be fully independent and self-reliant. And that is what they do. They grow up and they chart their own path in life. Isn't it possible that that is what could have happened?"

"I suppose so," said Benjamin still struggling with this prospect in his thoughts.

"There you go. Then it's settled. You have nothing to worry about. We are living in strange times being out here so far away from the old world. It's like humanity is always going in cycles. Living and reliving certain stages in our development as a species. Back before there was anyone here on Mars, the first settlers also had to make similar decisions that cut them off from ever returning to their homes and families. But that's just it. It's part of the human condition…"

"Honey," Mary intervened. "The man is hurting. I don't think it is the best time for a history lesson."

"It's not a history lesson. Simply a philosophy of life that we all have to be acquainted with. Especially us here on this far away outpost of humankind."

"I hear you, Joe," said Benjamin finally experiencing a short-term reprieve from his internal turmoil. A strange sense of peace, or resignation, had transformed his wild eyes and rapid speech. He was calm and deliberate with his words. He added:

"You sure do make a lot of sense. But just consider one thing. Isn't it strange how it seems that only the sons and daughters of common people like us are the ones who end up making these decisions to stay and never contact us again? The children of the rich always manage to make their way back home. Think about that four years from now when your kids *choose* to stay on Earth and you have no way to know what happened."

Benjamin and Joe became silent as they stared deeply into each other's eyes, both lost in their own thoughts, explanations, justifications, and logical reasoning for a puzzle too complicated for common people to solve.

All the while, from a corner of the hallway where they stood, the lens of a small camera peered over them capturing their interaction. At the receiving end of that connection in an undisclosed location of the Martian settlement, two individuals monitored the entire conversation, recording word for word. A third official came up to their station and retrieved from them a notepad with a list containing the names of the three individuals discussing the Earth-Mars Exchange program. The official noted their names on his own notepad on which were written a list of people and materials to be sent to Earth on the next available transfer.

Over 140 million miles away on a bright sunny day, a celebration was unfolding in the middle of Fifth Avenue in New York City. It was a parade commemorating the inauguration of the third ruler of America of the Roth dynasty. His name was John Jay Roth III. He was a boisterous, arrogant man full of bravado and incendiary rhetoric, who sought to break the last vestiges of resistance from the weak remnants of the United States Congress once and for all. He had come to power much like his family predecessors promising to root out all anti-American voices. All those civil rights advocates, feminists, and immigrant-loving liberals would no longer find refuge in the constitution claiming freedoms and rights not fully endorsed by the king himself. If they thought that his grandfather had been severe toward them, they had a truly rude awakening coming as soon as he took power.

That day, indeed, many had sought to protest the continued iron grip that the Roth dynasty held on the not-so-free press in America. But the Roth secret police had made sure to silence all descent. By the time of the commencement speech, no one dared to raise a single sign of protest or a loud chant against the new king. It was almost not even fun anymore. Or so John III would later say among his cabinet members.

There was no shortage of fans in attendance, cheering for the initiation of the new king's reign. As had become the tradition since the second election of his grandfather to the presidency of the United States, (prior to him declaring himself king), John J. Roth III would also stand right on Fifth Avenue, in front of the Roth Tower, and shoot someone before the eyes of his supporters, who had normalized the act to the extent that, instead of being horrified, they now spurred on their Kings in that macabre practice.

The convoy arrived from the landing site just in time for the ritual. The group of young people from Mars had been told that they were lucky to have arrived on that particular day, for it was the day of the inauguration of their new king. This did not seem odd to them at all, since they had grown up on Mars learning the history of the U.S. from text books written only from the start of the Roth dynastic rule. All other books were banned. People would hold public book-fueled bonfires when they confiscated books published prior to those dates. The ruling family's approved texts presented the words President and King as equal and interchangeable.

The Martians were led out of the vehicles one by one. In total, there were four at the celebration. The other arrivals had been taken to an undisclosed location for undisclosed and highly classified purposes. Among the four Martians were none other than Joe and Mary's son and daughter. They walked a long way toward the rendezvous point in front of Roth Tower. Along the way, they saw a multitude of people cheering and shouting at them. They were unsure how to gauge the crowd, though it did seem

122

that the euphoria of the masses was a bit overplayed. Or perhaps it was enhanced in some way either by alcohol or drugs or the fervor of the mob dynamic.

As they walked further along, the crowd began to tighten as more people filled the ranks and narrowed their passage. The hordes were frenetically eager to get near the Martians. They wanted to get a good look at the new arrivals. They wanted to touch them, come as close as possible to them, as if this would somehow grant them some benefit, like a benediction or simply good luck. The young Martians found it easy to get swept up in the fervor of such adulation, and soon found themselves granting the multitudes quick handshakes and light touches—and of course, plenty of smiles for their selfies in which they were asked to join. They felt like superstars. Something they would never have experienced on Mars.

When they reached the Roth Tower, King John Jay Roth III was standing there with his head held high. A wide grin of neither satisfaction nor happiness but simple smugness adorned his otherwise odious face. His hair, slicked back, shone bright in the sun like a golden helmet. He wore white gloves and a black classic long tailcoat. A meek-looking man stood beside this towering albino demagogue. In his hands was a box which he opened for King John III to choose his weapon of preference. As if choreographed, King John simply extended his hand sideways and to his back without looking at it to find the box containing the weapons. The attendant wisely surmised that it was incumbent upon him to ensure that the King found his target. So, he adjusted his place to help the King's hand fall on any gun, which he then gripped, swung

123

rapidly, and pointed it at the four Martians.

The crowd uttered a collective shushing sound, asking each other for silence as they saw King Roth III about to shoot. The four Martian youths upon seeing this gesture froze in their tracks not knowing if they should run or drop to their knees and plead for their lives. It would not have mattered, anyway. They were given no time to react. The gun blasted three times. The King was a marksman. He'd practiced religiously for this event. His grandfather, the first King of the U.S. would have been very proud.

As the blood began to soak the street, oozing out of the three dead Martians, the crowd exploded into wild cheers so loud that no one heard as the King shot the remaining bullets up into the air right above the head of the last Martian standing. It was Joe and Mary's daughter, Isabel. She was a beautiful thing. Clearly, the King had noticed her beauty, as well. No doubt he must have conjured other plans for her.

"What shall we do with the bodies, your highness?" asked the submissive attendant still standing next to the King.

"Add them to the barbecue. My people are hungry for justice," the King said dryly in an apparent attempt at a joke in spite of the fact that he meant what he said about literally feeding them to the mob.

"Very well, sir. And what about the girl?"

"I think I will taste her tonight, in my

124

chambers...And then tomorrow you can serve her in a nice little stew for the Russian president. Your people do quite enjoy your brown Martian meat. Isn't that so, Vlad?"

The King smiled sardonically as he said this. He tossed the gun aside for his lowly Russian servant to catch and proceeded to walk toward Isabel. As he approached, the King was brought to a halt by Isabel's screeching, terror-filled screams. It was as though she was just managing in that moment to break out of a gripping shellshock after seeing her brother and the others murdered in front of her. Her howl was so loud and terrifying that it even silenced the mob of Roth supporters for a split second in which they briefly saw Isabel's humanity on full display. But as the red caps began to rain upon them from the hands of the new King and his cabinet, the crowd quickly forgot about Isabel and the dead Martians. They eagerly extended their hands in the hopes of catching and donning one of those hats which were secretly made in Mexico.

Cannibal Rises

Julia was not the only woman to have become pregnant on the new planet. But it seemed she would be the one woman to give birth to the very first human-Martian baby. Unfortunately, complications arose. She lost her baby prematurely. There was nothing to be done to save him. The entire colony mourned for the mother, who was devastated, and for her baby (who, at least for some, represented something more than just being the first true Martian).

The pioneer colony was still so young that no one had died, either, so there were some considerations to be discussed when it came to the proper disposal of the fetal carcass. Prior pregnancies had not been faced with this question, since they had only resulted in the tiniest embryos.The parents moved quickly to suggest a Christian burial, and most of pioneers agreed. However, a small minority felt that burial was a practice of Earth where resources abounded. But on the barren, red planet everything was recycled for continued use, even their own urine. So, naturally, this was no exception. The carcass could represent a good source of nutrition for the struggling colonists whose only sources of food were vegetables grown in the greenhouse, nuts, some honey, and a few other canned goods which were on limited supply.

The parents were outraged at the implications,

especially Julia. They wanted to name their baby Victor, dress him as best they could, enjoy a quiet moment mourning him and send his soul off to heaven by setting him down into the ground to rest in peace.

"Soul? What soul? There is no such thing. Look around you. Look at where we are. Show me where you see the crosses, where you see the signs. Is God here? No!" said Mario, the colony technician and the most openly vocal on the topic.

"We are both Christians and we honor our heritage. We want to bury our child and pray that God receives him in heaven," retorted a mournful Julia.

"God, Christianity, a 'soul,' those are all things of Earth. Don't bring that over here," said Mario, directing his eyes at the others trying to appeal to them as they gathered around. "There is no God here. There isn't any God on Earth, either. When was the last time you saw God come down and light up a talking bush, huh? When was the last time God made a presence for his Christian worshipers on Earth? In more than two thousand years there have been no miracles, no walking on water, no frogs raining from the sky—nothing! This is all we got, friends. Just what we see, hear, touch, smell, and…taste. That's it."

"The fact that your faith is weak doesn't mean that we are crazy for believing in a higher power, Mario. We have a strong faith. We believe we will see our son in the next life." Sebastian spoke with a quiet dignity, the kind only a mournful father could project.

"Sebastian..." a woman called out to him, her voice rising from the crowd. "First of all, let me tell you that I fully agree with you. And I feel for the both of you...for your terrible loss. But I'm afraid that Mario does have a point. Everything on this planet must be decided upon by a majority vote in terms of if and how we could use, recycle, and reuse it. In this case it is an unfortunate reality, but one that the both of you know deep down we cannot simply pass over. Now, your baby was precious and worth saving if we had had the means to do so. But what happened to it was inevitable. It was just not meant to be for it to live to full-term. In a way, your baby was never even truly a baby at all. So, what does that make it after all? Can we truly consider it human if there was no birth?"

"How can you say that? How can you label our baby an 'it,' a thing! You animal. You evil bitch!" shouted Julia, seething with anger.

"Julia, please understand," said Mario. "We don't mean any disrespect. What we are proposing is not to defile the memory of your child but to use it—I mean, his body as a source of much needed food. Look at us. We are all deficient. We could all use a protein boost. That is exactly what your baby would do for us. Give life! I know I may have sounded insensitive when I countered your belief in God and your baby's afterlife. But my views are not what is important here. What is important is that you do believe in that higher power. As such you should be looking at this situation as a calling. Perhaps God has chosen you to deliver this unborn baby so that you, through him, can feed our faltering colony. Who knows, maybe this is the opportunity to survive just a few more days longer until we

128

are finally rescued. Isn't that a noble cause?"

"Please, everyone, let us be. Although as a father I feel a tremendous urge to lash out at all of you for proposing such a disturbing idea, and although I would not even come close to touching any food prepared off of the flesh of my kin, I do recognize that his body is simply that: flesh, and bone, and matter—only matter. His soul is no longer there. But give us some time to be with him and mourn together as a family as we come to terms with our sacrifice."

"But Sebastian, what are you saying? Have you lost your mind!"

"No, Julia. I am no crazier for accepting that conclusion as they are for proposing it in the first place. You know, as well as I, that what they have said is true. We grow hungrier and weaker by the day. It is not our right to keep them starving. It is the will of God that the colony eats of our son's body and live."

"Well, said, brother..." said Mario to no one in particular, since Sebastian completely ignored him, instead turning to console his wife. Mario looked at the couple trying to sound respectfully reassuring as he concluded with: "It's for the good of the colony. The greater good."

The couple retreated with their son, Victor, into the privacy of their living quarters to say their final farewells. After an hour, they handed over their baby's corpse to the hungry colonists. After a short ceremony, the carcass was dismembered so as to remove any traces of its humanity

129

and make it easier to cook and consume. Several of them, however, found it quite difficult to follow along with the plan to eat that baby. Those who did take part in the feasts managed to use the flesh sparingly in stews throughout a period of a few days. An unspoken agreement was reached that from that point on, whenever a fellow pioneer died of natural causes unrelated to disease, or in an accident, his or her body would be used as edible food. They thought it was their only shot at surviving.

One day, as the colonists took to their daily routines tending to the greenhouse gardens, and conducting equipment checks on the camp grounds someone noticed strange phenomena in the sky. At first, they appeared as specks in the distance. Then they began to notice streaks, what looked like lines of smoke lining the sky as the specks became larger. The pioneers realized that we were looking at hundreds of Mars landers. To some, it appeared to be an exodus from Earth.

Soon they verified that indeed that was the case. Earth had been consumed by all-out nuclear war. Before the apocalypse, many Earthlings were able to pay their way onto those ships that had transported them onto Martian lands. Of course, this meant that most of them were rich civilians, government officials, armed forces personnel, and all their families and attendants. At first, the pioneers were excited, for although it meant that Earth was gone forever, they at least had the company of many other humans now, including access to their resources.

The new arrivals had brought a few animals for possible domestication on Mars and for use as food sources. However, the animals did not fare well in the confined enclosures the immigrants had assembled to hold them. They asked the pioneers how it was that they were able to survive as long as they had without the use of animals as sources of protein. When they learned of the pioneers' cannibalistic practices, the immigrants were stunned. They separated themselves to another outpost, labeling the pioneers as "primitive savages, and seizing any further contact. The new world order existed as such for nearly a year until, finally, an envoy of immigrants was sent back to the original colony to seek out the pioneers.

For their part, the pioneers were happy to host the immigrants again as guests with as much amenities as they could provide, given that they had close to nothing. The envoy looked nervous and jumpy. They seemed to be taking in the surroundings as if assessing the place somehow. Sure enough, two days after they returned to their settlement, a convoy of military men and women were sent to capture every last pioneer and take them to the new colony. Once there, they were all steered into a very large room in one of the holding facilities. A man wearing a Mars Four Corporation logo as a badge on his suit entered and spoke over the crowds as if addressing creatures who were incapable of thought or human communication. He said,

"This group shall be properly cared for by residents from sector C-13. The beasts shall be well fed, and their health carefully monitored. Harsh penalties will be implemented upon anyone who disregards these protocols. Let it be duly noted that this has been decreed and shall become the law forever."

A man of smaller stature came out from behind the official and quickly noted his words onto a notepad and followed like a dog as the official extended his hand pointing to several young people among the pioneers. He then whispered something to his attendant, who in turn relayed an order to two armed guards who went in to retrieve them. The guards began plucking out the young men and women from among the crowd, directing them toward a door which was close by. At that point, the official, who had directed the guards from a raised platform exited the room, leaving the pioneers staring at each other in bewilderment. Suddenly the door to the raised platform swung open once again and this time there was a woman standing where the previous official had stood dictating their decree. The woman looked down at the pioneers and said:

"The beasts will take off their clothes entirely and without protest."

Confused, the pioneers simply looked around at each other as if no one understood the command. The woman again spoke saying:

"The animals will remove their clothing immediately or face their due punishment!"

Someone from the crowd finally mustered the courage to utter the words on the minds of all of the men and women in the group:

"What is happening? What is this all about? We are

132

the first colonists. Why do we have to remove our clothes?"

Before she could respond, another anonymous voice shouted,

"We demand to be released at once!"

The woman furiously stared down at the man who dared to raise his voice and shouted:

"Get it!"

A group of men entered the large enclosure and apprehend the man. It turned out to be none other than Mario, the outspoken one. The woman shouted down at them collectively:

"This will be the first and only time that we will address you all as if you were anything other than cattle. Observe the consequence of disobedience."

As she said this she pointed to Mario who was instantly disemboweled by the guards and left to die on the floor as a prey animal seeing his insides ripped out of his body.

"You all will have a choice on how to die. For those who are compliant, you will be treated with care and given good food and all the comforts that we can provide. For those who chose to speak up, or speak at all, even amongst yourselves, your punishment will be ten times as harsh as it was for your fellow man lying there in his own blood and guts. This is the order of things now. There is no other way.

The survival of our species depends upon the strict following of one course of action. We will not be deterred. From now on, you will obey our commands without failure and without questioning."

She paused to look at the pioneers, who by then had lost all signs of humanity, and had turned to beasts for sacrifice in her eyes. She continued saying,

"As for your offspring...that is, when we begin breeding your kind, they will be properly cared for. They will be paired up and bred, as well. They will provide our colony an ample supply of cattle for sustenance and labor. But do not be saddened, at least they will not be the first to be butchered. You will have that honor."

When she was done dictating to them, she seemed to simply flip a switch which allowed her to revert back to an automaton who no longer saw them as beings to communicate with, but instead shouted instructions and commands at her enforcers who eagerly obeyed. She turned around and exited the door which, as it shut behind her, made a loud clicking sound and an electrical hum ensued. The lights shut off as the pioneers, who were now fully nude, were left huddling in the uncertainty of a new reality, waiting to be sacrificed for the greater good.

#ZombieApocalypse

"Bring me the Martian ones back home," the President stated emphatically as he took his seat in the Oval Office. "No matter the cost. The people demand a feel-good story. They want to feel like they are wining again! By bringing back the Martian colonists we will boost our nation's morale, which will get us a step closer out of this recession."

His audience of one was a NASA official who was in charge of briefing the President on anything involving the Mars Four Corporation's colonization efforts (in partnership with NASA) on Mars.

"Mr. President," said the NASA official. "There is just one thing to consider before bringing back the crew, sir."

"What's that?"

"That it may not be at all possible to accommodate them anywhere in the public sphere other than at one of our maximum-security facilities...uh, to contain any possible contagion, sir."

"Well that won't work. I need them to be accessible to the American people. Americans need to be able to not only see them but touch them and stand next to them taking selfies and all. You get me?"

"Yes, sir, Mr. President. Absolutely I understand. But there is," the NASA official hesitated briefly, "...a very critical issue at hand that we just cannot be certain how to handle."

"What exactly are you talking about?"

"Well, we have discovered a certain kind of...what seems like...a bug."

"A bug? How's that possible? I thought you nerdy scientist-types agreed there was no life on that planet."

"Technically there isn't, sir," the official said coyly as he adjusted his undersized sports jacket and straightened his bifocals.

"...You see, what we have discovered is what you could essentially call a fossil. It could present a problem when exposed to Earth atmosphere."

"Ok, let me get this straight. You are worried that a *fossil* will present a problem here on Earth. But who the hell asked you to bring back any fossils from Mars? I specifically told you to bring back the Martian colonists only."

"Oh, of course, sir. My apologies for not explaining myself thoroughly. See, these fossils are essentially microscopic and, what's worse, they are ubiquitous."

"What the hell does that mean? Speak to me in plain English, damnit! What exactly is the problem!"

136

"Well, sir, it means they are microscopic and there are so many that they are practically everywhere on the Martian atmosphere. The fact that they are so tiny is what presents a problem, since they can literally penetrate any suit or equipment our astronauts use on Mars. We are almost certain that these microscopic 'fossils' will also be present on or even inside the colonists themselves. And the problem with that, sir, is that these critters might not be fossils altogether...They might be a kind of living dead organism."

The President had so-far exercised some restraint, allowing the NASA official to voice their concerns. But the last statement made the President's blood boil. He lashed out at the official saying,

"What kind of sci-fi bullshit have you brought to me today? You expect me to scrap these plans based on your weak evidence about some goddamn microscopic fossil from Mars? Get the fuck out of here!"

"Forgive me, Mr. President but I feel that I must give you a full accounting of exactly what it is that we are worried about, sir. See, as I mentioned, they appear as fossils to us only because it seems they have been inactive for who knows how long. But there is another theory floating around among our scientists..."

The official paused as he noticed the President quite visibly losing all remaining patience. He began to breath loudly, spreading his nostrils wide and tightening his lips. This produced what would have appeared to the gullible as a smile, but in actuality, it was the President's way of inadvertently announcing that he was about to rise to his feet and charge on them, like a demon bull. The official had seen that reaction before so he knew he didn't have much more time with the President.

He sped up his report saying, "In closing, some scientists have noted that there is reason to believe those microbes to be in a hibernation-state. There is no telling if they went into hibernation after the end of life-bearing conditions on Mars, or if they are recent arrivals who would be totally revived here on Earth, since they are--or were at one point--carbon-based beings dependent on oxygen, water, and other conditions that give life it's impetus."

"Look here, you two-bit scientist nerd. There is no way this mission is going to be stopped by some pansy-ass, pencil neck like yourself. You listen to me carefully, and listen good. You will say nothing to anyone else about what we discussed here today, you got it? Because if you do...," the President threatened as he rose to his feet and reached across, grabbing the official by the neck tie pulling him closer until he had him splayed across the Presidential desk, "I will make sure that you and everyone you love are thrown into the darkest, ugliest hole in the ground where no one will ever hear your screams and nobody will know of you again. And I will personally come pay you a visit every birthday and major holiday you got left in your miserable nerd life just to ram my foot all the way up your ass. You got that!!!"

"Yes, sir. Y-yes, Mr. President, sir," responded the official, the fright having caused the blood from his skin to

138

retreat, leaving him looking pale, shuddering, and unable to breath properly.

What was most horrifying to the official was the graveness in the severity of the President's threat. He believed every word of it. He knew the President had meant what he said in the most literal sense. He was certain inasmuch as he had seen it in the abyss of the President's eyes, where there was nothing, not even a soul, but only darkness. The wide-eyed official trembled as he slowly stepped backwards towards the door waiting for the President to dismiss him with the usual wave of his hand.

The rest of the tragic tale about the first outbreak of the unknown virus played out like a series on television. The first stage of the outbreak started with the President on a public news conference welcoming the Martian colonists. For television viewers, it may have appeared quite normal with the exception of the awkward, lethargic movements of the Martian colonists. They all seemed dumbstruck...static; as if they had trouble hearing the President as he welcomed them home, trying to shake their hands. They hardly smiled. The reporters vied against each other fervently trying to get the exclusive, but the Martians ones simply stood there, completely disinterested, looking past them.

News correspondents on-site stood stiff, bewildered at what was unfolding. Some looked at the cameramen shooting live and at their producers for direction. They soon realized that there was no option but to turn it back to anchorwomen or men at their corresponding studios. The anchors quickly had to bring in so-called experts, specialists, and doctors--anyone whom they might have standing-by to comment as to why the Martians seemed to be acting so strangely. The doctors and specialists had similar diagnoses: the Martians were quite possibly experiencing a certain kind of space lag, and some mild version of PTSD after having been on Mars for two years and suddenly being brought back to Earth.

The second stage of the outbreak followed with TV camera crews capturing images of the Martians being paraded through Fifth Avenue in New York. Then a scene of chaos erupted after the astronauts collapsed in the middle of the procession, seemingly affected simultaneously by something in the air. Emergency personnel attended them immediately. They seemed to recover but something about them didn't look right. They began to attack the emergency responders, then the public at large. Everyone started running for their lives, trampling each other and the camera crews who were still filming the unfolding panic in the streets. Police officers pulled their guns and unloaded them on the Martian crew at will, but they seemed immune to bullets and, therefore, unstoppable. They overwhelmed the police. The people they attacked fell dead but then got back up after some moments and joined the Martians in attacking all living humans.

Back at the White House in Washington, an aide to the President came urgently running down the hall toward the oval office. He knocked rapidly and entered before getting the go ahead. The aide had a message of national security importance, therefore, the President would understand him taking the liberty to let himself in... or so he hoped. He found the President sitting on his chair seemingly looking out the window as if in deep contemplation.

"Mr. President. I have urgent news," said the aide at the back of the chair which completely concealed the President's head. All he could see was the Commander in Chief's bare knees, which protruded through the bathrobe he was wearing.

"There has been an incident on Fifth Avenue, sir. There is chaos spreading everywhere. What should we do? The generals have asked us to get your approval to enact martial law so they can go in and quell the mayhem."

The aide moved closer. As he did this, he noticed the President holding his phone in his hand, and on the screen the aide spotted the President's Twitter profile. He apparently was in the middle of a tweet. But his thumb seemed to hesitate to finish the message and post it.

"Sir...," the aide said, slowly inching toward his boss. "Mr. President?"

The President remained silent. The aide reached the chair, and noticed the leader of the free world seemingly frozen in his seat. He delicately touched the backrest to swivel the chair around to face him. As he did, he noticed that the President looked strange. A festering, orange slime oozed down most of his face and his eyes had a greenish hue. Those eyes seemed to be looking past the aide and off into space. Dead. But suddenly they readjusted and stared straight at the official.

Without warning, the President (or the thing that used to be the Commander in Chief of the United States) leapt from the chair tackling the aide to the floor and devouring his face. Soon the aide, too, had turned into a deformed--beyond dead, but not quite living--creature bearing all his teeth as the flesh from his face, including his nose, were gone. White House staff and cabinet members found themselves under attack by the aide and the now Zombie-in-Chief, as he walked down the halls, bathrobe wide open, exposing his naked body in search of the living. On the screen of his phone, which was still gripped in one hand, was the Twitter feed trending:

#ZombieApocolypse

Bonus Track: Astro Zombies

The zombie hordes had nearly killed off or turned all of humanity into undead corpses. Had it not been for a zombie attack at the Space Center in Houston, the aimlessly-meandering dead would never have realized that the remaining humans had devised a way to save humanity from total extinction by transporting as many people out of Earth on spaceships, and establishing cities on the moon, where they could have a fresh start away from the threat of the zombie virus.

The zombies looked for a spaceship of their own (for these zombies were of the thinking kind) to follow the humans into the sky. But since they were zombies, after all, they did not know how to fly the spaceship. So, when they started the rocket they burned to a crisp their buddies who were standing right under the propulsion system. After they cleared the area, the mission control zombies gave the okay to launch again. The go-ahead came with the signal of two putrefying thumbs way up from the control tower. However, when the astronaut zombies (we'll call them astro-zombies) lifted off, they didn't get far. They didn't even get as high as a cumulus cloud, because one of them pushed a lever when he should have pulled it so, he ended up driving the nose of the rocket down into the ground where it exploded into bits.

The mission control zombies were furious at the apparent ineptitude of their own species when they saw this happen. Frustrated, they threw their papers in the air, and removed their head pieces impetuously—accidentally ripping off their own ears in the process—throwing them on the floor, and stomping on them saying "aaarrrghh!!!" They seemed to become even more agitated at the fact that they could not fully express their rage, because they could not speak any language whatever. Otherwise, they would have cursed a healthy dose of all the bad words that their hearts desired. It took what, to them, felt like an eternity (since they move at turtle speed), but eventually they found another rocket. This time the zombie technicians knew not to stand right under the vessel if they wanted to avoid being charred by the engines.

The astro-zombies were finally able to take off, this time flying past the highest cirrus clouds. Their ship flew further up until they exited Earth's blue sky allowing them to enter the blackness of space. They cheered as they high-fived one another accidentally snapping and breaking off hands or fingers in their excitement.

While in space the astro-zombies were awed by the beauty of the stars and planets. But a rumble in their bellies reminded them that the reason they were in space in a rocket ship was not to admire the cosmos but to look for humans to eat!

Suddenly, they saw a light blinking on the control panel and heard an indicator ting. The ship was running out of fuel! It seemed that they had been much more captivated by the awesome nature of space than they realized, and had totally missed their turn, going straight past the moon all the way to Mars. The astro-zombies had to make an emergency crash-landing on the red planet, since by then they were simply gliding on pure momentum. Luckily for them, they all survived the crash…well, at least partially. Some of them survived from the waist up, others only missing one or one and a half limbs. So, a few of them had to hop around as they all went looking for something to do. Now, not only were they stranded without a ship, they also still had no humans on whom to feed. They were starving on Mars with no way out.

After walking and hopping aimlessly, they came into a canyon where they saw a great city beyond, and thought that for sure now they would be saved from starvation. Certainly, the existence of a city meant the presence of mouthwatering, live human beings. So, they went down to the city hopping, skipping, and walking as awkwardly as zombies do, but when they got there and saw the beings that came out to greet them, they were quite disappointed to see that they were not humans but aliens!

The aliens came forward to greet them by shaking hands, thinking these were regular "men in black" types, the kind of humans with whom they had dealt before. But the astro-zombies were so hungry that, instead of shaking hands, they bit off some of the alien's fingers. These were no delicacies, like human fingers, but beggars can't be choosers. The aliens were so angered at this that, although they could easily regrow their chewed off digits like Mexican Axolotl salamanders, they brought out their laser guns and zapped the astro-zombies instantly disintegrating them where they stood. But by then it was too late, because the zombie virus had begun spreading throughout their Martian colony. The virus traveled rapidly among them since they were joined by an invisible matter that

146

encapsulated them all, like living together in a bubble. The fortunate thing for them was that as aliens their zombie versions were not as dull as human zombies, so the zombie aliens flew their ships to the moon to find the humans, whom they thought had been the ones to send those astro-zombies to their Martian base. But once there a human they randomly encountered said,

"No. We didn't send those zombies to Mars to get you. We would never do that!"

One of the alien zombies said, "Ok, then. Take me to your leader."

The person took the Martian visitor to a woman from the Lunar base, and the alien zombie asked her:

"Are you the human leader?"

"Yes, I am," said the woman.

"Well good to meet you!" said the alien zombie extending his hand for the woman to shake.

When the leader of the humans put her hand out, the alien zombie said,

"By the way, it is our custom to kiss the hand that we are about to shake…"

"Ok," said the woman hesitantly.

The alien zombie took her hand and went to kiss it,

147

but instead bit off two of the human leader's fingers instantly transforming her into a zombie. She, in turn, began attacking all her cabinet until every one of them had turned into zombies. However, before the zombified leader and her cabinet could go rampaging throughout the Lunar base annihilating the remnants of humanity, the alien zombies, still preserving some wisdom and forethought (for if the humans were extinct, they would have no one else to abduct but those zombie dummies back on Earth), decided to abduct the entire Lunar base's zombie leadership.

The zombie aliens realized that they had to come up with a solution to the destructiveness of the zombie hunger that had finished off all humanity on Earth. So, they decided to take the zombie leader and her cabinet back to Earth and resettle them among the entirely zombified population of that planet. As a solution to the hunger crisis unfolding on Earth since the decimation of all living animal species, the alien zombies offered them a zapping gun that shot a laser at anything to which the human zombies pointed turning it into an animal of their choice to eat. It provided them with every living thing to eat, except humans. In that way, the zombies would be able to convert stones and other inanimate objects, which are in abundance, into living things to eat. However, since they were still human zombies and, therefore, very dumb, they sometimes zapped themselves, turning into chickens or cows and running away from their hungry buddies who could no longer distinguish between a zombie friend and a venerable feast.

GABRIEL HUGO SPRUNG INTO EXISTENCE FULLY
FORMED WITH THE TOOLS OF WRITING IN HIS
HANDS. HE SPAWNED FROM THE WOMB OF AN
ANGEL FROM ANOTHER GALAXY WHO HAS
RETURNED TO HER HOME PLANET LEAVING HIM
TO EXPLORE THIS EARTH UNTIL HIS DAY COMES
TO JOIN HIS KIND.

For more visit: **http://gabrielhugo.info**